All I Want
for Christmas

All I Want for Christmas

Wendy Loggia

Underlined

Text copyright © 2020 by Wendy Loggia
Jacket art copyright © 2020 by Josie Portillo

All rights reserved. Published in the United States by Underlined, an imprint of Random House Children's Books, a division of Penguin Random House LLC, New York.

Underlined is a registered trademark and the colophon is a trademark of Penguin Random House LLC.

GetUnderlined.com

Educators and librarians, for a variety of teaching tools, visit us at RHTeachersLibrarians.com

Library of Congress Cataloging-in-Publication Data is available upon request.
ISBN 978-0-593-17983-3 (paperback) — ISBN 978-0-593-17984-0 (ebook)

The text of this book is set in 12-point Adobe Jenson.
Interior design by Ken Crossland

Printed in the United States of America
10 9 8 7 6 5 4 3 2 1
First Edition

For Olivia & Will

1

Christmas Wrapping

I should realize it's a bad sign when I trip hard over the entry to Winslow's Bookshop.

"Whaaaaa!" I yelp as I give the typically sticky front door my customary push . . . and unexpectedly go flying into the store, the shop's brass bell announcing my unceremonious entrance.

"Carl finally put a little oil on that door so we don't have to work so hard to get in here," Victoria, the owner of Winslow's, says, looking up at me with a bemused smile. Nothing ruffles her. She's on her knees, putting a stack of books on a wooden shelf. "Hope you didn't hurt yourself."

My eyes dart around. Luckily the only people to witness my epic fall are Victoria, who has the decency not to laugh in my face; a mom preoccupied on her phone while pushing a baby stroller; and Victoria's basset hound, Fred. He gazes balefully at me, a pair of reindeer antlers perched on his large head.

"Nope, I'm fine." I take in a deep breath. "Ahhh, my favorite smell: peppermint, pine cones, and new books." I'd started working at Winslow's last summer, and despite what my friends who lifeguarded, camp-counseled, and taught dance thought, bookselling was the best summer job ever. I've actually been lucky enough to stay on part-time during the school year. Victoria and her husband, Carl, own the bookshop and they are supercool. Everyone who works here loves to read and talk about books. Winslow's is a popular place in our town for people to come and spend time. It is, as Victoria likes to say, a community.

Victoria is always encouraging us to take books home to read. "Read more, sell more," she'll say, handing me copies of the latest romances (my favorite). The store also runs a mystery book club and an award-winner book club, and it has tons of events for kids. There are strands of twinkly lights, comfy chairs filled with pillows, old wooden bookshelves worn smooth from years of use, and a café in the back that sells the most delicious panini and acai bowls and gives us a 20 percent employee discount.

If I could live here, I would.

Victoria stands up, a pair of pink tassel earrings swinging from her ears. "You're not scheduled to work tonight, are you?" she asks, her brow puckering.

I shake my head. "Wrapping." I've been averaging around ten hours a week at the store this fall, but tonight I am here strictly in a volunteer capacity. Each holiday season, Victoria and Carl invite students from my school, Bedford High, to staff the wrapping station and accept donations. All the money goes to support the arts at our school, and I'd signed up for a weekly shift.

"Ahhh, right." Victoria clasps her hands together. "Okay, off to special-order *The Atlas of Amazing Birds* for a young naturalist before I forget. Coffee's made in the back if you want a cup." She walks off. "French hazelnut," she calls over her shoulder before I can ask.

In the staff room in the back, I shrug out of my blue parka and pink scarf and pull out my light-up Christmas bulb necklace from my GOT BOOKS? tote bag.

"Ah, there she is, Miss Bailey Briggs, a cup of Christmas cheer." My coworker Bill bustles past me, a pencil behind his ear and a coffee mug in his hand, his standard white cotton shirt rumpled as usual. Originally from Ireland, and about the same age as my grandpa, Bill is as much a fixture in the store as the comfy sofas in the Fiction section and Fred at the cash register. And with his heavy Irish brogue, he is one of the most popular readers at Saturday Storytime.

"Hi, Bill," I greet him. "Did you finish that mystery you were reading last week? The one about a murder in Dublin?"

He chuckles. "I did, I did. Already on to the next in the series. I'm addicted, I am, Bailey. Tana French. You should give her a read."

I pull on my plush Santa hat and arrange my hair. "Not my thing, Bill. Sorry."

"I know, I know. You want what all the young girls want. A loooooove story." He gives me a dismissive wave.

3

Even though I find his attitude slightly patronizing, I have to admit he's right—at least when it comes to me. I *do* want a love story. Specifically, a Christmas one. A sweet one, filled with snuggles under blankets and hot chocolate and text messages filled with red and green hearts and Santa emojis. I've watched more than my fair share of Hallmark Christmas movies, and even though I'm not a big-city lawyer who has moved back to my hometown to save the family business or a world-weary writer who falls in love with a recently widowed baker, I still believe in the power of Christmas Magic.

A holiday romance is in my future.

At least a girl can dream.

And it isn't like I don't have something to back my dream up. I meet two of the main criteria for a cheesy Christmas romance:

1. I work in a bookshop.
2. I was dumped, although not that recently.

I dated Oliver Moreno for four months before I found out that he wanted to just "be friends" because he had kissed Kate Collins, a sophomore in the marching band. The kiss took place after the winter concert, and apparently it was life-changing.

Whatever. Oliver isn't that great a kisser, if I'm being honest. Kate can have him.

But see, that isn't the point. I don't just want someone

4

to kiss. I want someone to experience Christmas Magic with me. Christmas Magic begins the moment Santa appears at the end of the Macy's Thanksgiving Day Parade. That's when the holiday season always starts—the season of cookie baking and tree trimming, sledding and snowfalls, Secret Santas and eggnog and Christmas songs on every radio station. It really is the most wonderful time of the year.

And what I really want for Christmas is something I probably would never admit to anyone. Not to my friends, and definitely not to my sister. It's honestly hard to even swallow my pride and admit it to myself.

But here it is: I want to be kissed underneath the mistletoe by someone who really thinks I'm amazing.

That's it. That's my Christmas wish.

I don't think it's too much to ask for.

But will it ever come true?

. . .

"Snowmen or snowflakes?" I smile up at the college-aged guy standing in front of my gift-wrap station.

He doesn't answer me. Instead, he drops a heap of books on the table with a loud *thunk*. I pick up the top one. It's a cookie cookbook. "OMG, this looks delicious," I say, flipping to a recipe for salted chocolate chunk cookies. "Or should I say . . . *dough*licious?"

My wrapping partner, Sam Gorley, laugh-snorts beside

me. "It must be time to go home, because I'm actually starting to find your jokes funny." She yawns. "Or maybe I'm just
tired." Sam is in my grade at school. We aren't really in the
same friend group—she hangs out mostly with the band
kids—but since we started volunteering at the gift-wrap
station, we've become kind of friendly. She spends a lot of
time posting on social media and showing me pictures of
her cat, Meow.

We've been wrapping for three hours now, and we're
starting to get a little silly.

I turn back to the customer, who is staring at the giant
rolls of wrapping paper. "So what'll it be?" I am very into
themes, especially when they involve the holidays, and holiday baking is one thing I'm always in favor of. So a guy
buying a cookie cookbook as a gift makes me happy. Maybe
he's going to surprise his girlfriend with homemade sugar
cookies. Or maybe he has a little brother he wants to teach
how to bake in time for Saint Nick. I smile, imagining the
heartwarming kitchen scene.

He cuts me off mid-fantasy, frowning. "Uh . . . do you
have something a little less . . . Christmas?"

I can't stop myself. I frown back. *Less* Christmas? Less
Christmas is right up there with No-Egg Easter and Fire-
crackerless Fourth, obviously a phrase that would never
pass my lips, but I try to maintain my professional com-
posure even though I'm wearing a plush red Santa hat and
a strand of blinking lights from Five Below around my
neck. "Oh, sure," I say smoothly, reaching under the table

and hoisting up a roll of wrapping paper. The rolls are even heavier than they look. "We don't have room on the table for all our choices. Here's another Happy Hanukkah . . . and we also have Dogs in Stockings."

He shakes his head, his shaggy bangs covering his eyes. "Nah. How about something purple?"

I stare at him. "As in red meets blue?"

He nods. "Yeah. Purple."

I'm about to object when Sam awakes from her nap and whips into action. "Here you go, sir," she says, grabbing the books and wrapping them in a flurry of white tissue paper. She puts them in a fancy cream-colored WINSLOW'S bag, slaps a gold foil sticker on it, and ties it up with a purple ribbon that she apparently pulled out of thin air. "Happy holidays!"

"Cool. Thanks." He pushes a couple bucks into the donation jar and heads out the door, the little bells dinging upon his exit.

Sam turns to me and holds up her hand in anticipation of what I'm about to say. "Don't even start."

My shoulders rise and fall. "I just don't understand people," I say sadly. "Purple? For Christmas?"

Sam's scrolling rapidly through her texts. "Not everyone's as into the holidays as you are, Bailey."

"So I've noticed," I tell her, dejectedly picking at the fuzz on my red wool sweater.

"Anyway, are you going to that party tomorrow night at Joe's house?" she asks, not looking up from her phone.

I shake my head. "I don't even know what you're talking about."

Sam sighs in the overly dramatic manner I've come to know well these past few weeks. "Joe Shiffley invited a bunch of people over to hang out. You should come."

I shrug. "Maybe." I don't even know Joe, so the idea of showing up at his house for a party feels very awkward.

No one is coming over to the gift-wrap table. Sam heads to the restroom, and while she's gone, I decide to rearrange everything. I line up the ribbon spools on the left—green, red, white, blue, silver—and put the tape dispenser next to them, along with a giant pair of scissors, a candle jar we now use to hold pens, and two gigantic rolls of paper. I pick up all the stray bits of cut ribbon from the floor and fluff the money in the donation jar.

When the bell at the shop's entrance rings, I glance over. And when I see who it is, my eyebrows shoot up. It's Jacob Marley, this guy from my grade at school. We were in biology together in ninth grade. The main reason I know him is because he had gone out with this girl, Jessica Dolecki, that I dislike. She has thick wavy blond hair, a pushed-up nose, and a high-pitched laugh, and she always wears a Canada Goose jacket. I think Jacob is on the track team—or maybe he's a wrestler?—but other than that, I don't really know him. He's wearing dark track pants, sneakers, a gray sweatshirt, and a Boston Red Sox cap.

He lifts his chin in my direction. "Hey, Bailey."

"Hey," I say back, giving him an awkward wave. I'm a little surprised that he knows who I am.

"Nice hat," he says, smirking. "Goes with the necklace."

"Why, thank you," I say, adjusting the white furry rim while ignoring the fact that what he said is most likely not a compliment.

"So, uh, you work here?"

I shrug. "I do, actually. But tonight I'm just here to wrap."

He laughs, and a dimple in his right cheek makes an appearance. "Never would have guessed you and Drake had something in common."

"I never would have guessed I'd see you in a bookstore on a Friday night," I retort before I can stop myself.

He shoves his hands into his pockets. "What's that supposed to mean?"

"Oh, um, I don't know," I say feebly, feeling my cheeks pinken. Why did I say that? He doesn't exactly seem like the reading type, but really, I don't even know Jacob. That sounded a lot meaner than I meant it to.

"So, yeah, I'm doing some shopping. For Christmas."

Something in my heart gives a little flip. Any boy who comes to a bookstore for Christmas shopping gets bonus points. Now I feel extra bad that I insulted him. Most boys I know give gift cards for presents—if they even give a gift. Oliver and I weren't together at Christmas, but something tells me he would definitely have been the gift-card type. Or, if I'm being honest, the no-gift type.

"And so you came in here," I say, stating the obvious.

He nods. "Would you want to help me?" He holds up his phone. "I've got a list."

"Oh," I say, surprised. "I mean, I'm not technically working now but . . ." Known fact about me here at Winslow's: giving people book advice is my thing. There's something about matching the right book with the right reader, putting the right book into a customer's hands: I love it. And helping a customer like Jacob is extra-satisfying, like watching my parents master a TikTok dance I've taught them.

I'm in.

Sam's back from the restroom. Her thick eyebrows skyrocket above her black framed glasses as she takes a look at Jacob. I'm sure she recognizes him from school and is probably just as surprised as I am to see him inside Winslow's.

"Um, I'm going to help this customer with his shopping," I say, taking Jacob by the arm and ushering him swiftly away before Sam starts asking him questions. She's one of those people who can talk forever—and we only have an hour before the store closes. Standing by the Poetry section, we huddle together over his iPhone as I read the list.

"Hmmm. Okay. Mom. Dad. Little brother. Grandma," I mumble, making a mental checklist of Jacob's family and what they might be like. "Very doable."

He puts his phone in his back pocket, and for a second I think I see a flicker of something—surprise? apprehension?—flash over his face. But then he's smiling at me before I can comment on it, and then I'm not sure it was even there at all. Boys are weird.

I escort him over to the cookbooks—probably one of the most popular sections in the store during the holidays. "Does your mom watch *Face the Nation* or *Real Housewives?*" I ask. "Or is she more of a podcast person?"

"Uh, *Real Housewives*, I think?" Jacob says, looking confused. He chews on his bottom lip, which is already chapped. "What does that have to do with anything?"

"Entertainment preferences tell me a lot about a person," I say. I pull a copy of Chrissy Teigen's *Cravings* off the shelf and hand it to him.

"You didn't even ask if my mom cooks, though," he says, raising an eyebrow. His eyes are the steely blue of an Alaskan husky, and I find myself looking at them—or, rather, into them—for a second longer than I should.

Don't get sucked in, I tell myself. I'm pretty sure that Jacob Marley is a bit of a player. He hangs with a loud, semi-obnoxious crowd, he always seems to have an answer for everything, and he went out with Jessica Dolecki, so he obviously has questionable judgment. Certainly not who I imagine kissing under the mistletoe.

I tear my gaze away from his Alaskan husky eyes. "Doesn't matter. Everyone loves looking at beautiful food. And this one actually has great recipes. There's one for ramen salad that'll blow your mind."

"Wow. Okay," he says agreeably. "That sounds amazing."

I smile, imagining his mom opening it up on Christmas. *You're welcome, Jacob.*

We move over to the Performing Arts section of the shop. There's a round table stacked with books ranging from dance to theater to music. It's what Victoria calls an impulse stop.

"My dad likes rock," Jacob says, and I get the sense he hadn't realized there were actually books about musicians. He points to a Pearl Jam trivia book. "This could be cool."

I nod encouragingly. "I was going to suggest a biography—dads love them. Prince, Tom Petty, The Rock . . ."

Jacob picks up *Acid for the Children* by Flea. "My dad likes the Chili Peppers," he muses, thumbing through the pages.

"Winner winner chicken dinner," I say, then cover my mouth. My dad is the king of corny expressions, and sadly, I have picked up a few of them. But Jacob doesn't seem to think it's strange. He just laughs.

"You're pretty good at this book stuff," he says approvingly. "You know, it's almost like you work here or something." He is standing just close enough for me to smell him: a mix of Downy fabric softener and wet dog. It's more appealing than you would think. But then I remind myself that holiday dreams are made of peppermint, evergreen, and cedar.

"Yeah, you know, I try," I say modestly, but the truth is,

I am pretty proud of my book-matching skills. I was even Employee of the Month back in July, and my shelftalkers—the little signs we're encouraged to put under books we love with short write-ups of why we love them—are customer favorites.

"Now, my little bro, Preston, is kind of a tough one," he says, stroking his chin. "He's not really into reading. He likes to play lacrosse and video games."

The not-reading thing is something I hear a lot from customers, especially parents, and about boys. "You just have to find the right book," I tell him with conviction as I lead him to the Kids' section at the back of the store. We browse through fantasy, sports fiction, and graphic novels, finally settling on *A Wolf Called Wander*, about a wolf cub that has to find a new home, and the Trials of Apollo series by Rick Riordan because Jacob remembered reading another series by the author when he was in middle school and liking it.

Music begins playing, and I recognize Kelsea Ballerini's version of "My Favorite Things." The floor is pretty crowded now, and there's definitely a feeling of Christmas spirit in the air.

"So now all we have left is Grandma," I say, rubbing my hands together. "Cozy mystery? Sudoku puzzle book? Mindfulness mantras? Talk to me."

He rocks lightly on his feet, considering the options. "Gram's a pretty curious person," he finally says. "She audits classes at her local community college just for fun, ballroom dances with her boyfriend, Rocco, and goes out for mimosas with her friends every Sunday."

"My kind of lady," I say with true admiration. After some back-and-forth, we settle on Mo Rocca's *Mobituaries*, about lives well-lived. It's popular with the over-forty crowd.

"She'll love it," Jacob says, reading the description on the inside flap. "Thanks, Bailey. You really helped me."

"Sure thing," I say, suddenly feeling awkward now that our reason for hanging out together is coming to a close. "Anytime." I look toward the cash register. "If you, uh, want to go and pay for everything, I can wrap it when you're done."

A flush spreads over Jacob's face. "Uh, yeah. About that. I, um, I kind of forgot my wallet."

I stare at him. "Say what?"

He nods, looking uncomfortable. "Yeah. I realized it when I put my phone in my pocket."

"And you . . . just decided to keep shopping?" I say, confused. "Were you going to pay with your phone?" My mind flashes to the guys he hangs out with at school. I could totally imagine them working with a personal shopper and then just walking out for the fun of it. Which apparently is what Jacob is planning on doing today.

"No," he says, looking a little embarrassed. "I don't have it set up."

"Oh. So . . . how were you going to pay?" I ask, leaving the question hanging in the air.

"I . . . yeah. I guess I didn't think it through. You seemed so into helping me that I, uh, didn't want to disappoint you."

Disappoint me? Clearly he thinks I set a very low bar for excitement. And maybe I do, which makes me even more annoyed than I should be. I fold my arms across my chest. "That was thirty minutes of my life I can't get back now. Thanks a lot."

"You seemed like you were having fun, though," he tells me sheepishly. He gives me a hangdog expression—the kind I'm sure has worked for him before. "I'll come back with my wallet to get these. I promise."

"Sure you will," I say in a monotone, sounding like the cafeteria lady at school when someone in the line "forgets" their swipe card.

"No, seriously," he says, scrolling on his phone and then heading toward the door. Obviously something more exciting has come up. "I will. See ya, Bailey."

I lift my hand in the most unenthusiastic wave possible. As bizarre as it seems, I think maybe I was wondering, in my deep subconscious, if Jacob Marley *could* be mistletoe-worthy. But now that I know he wasn't taking any of this seriously—or more precisely, taking me and my time seriously—um, no.

That little flip my heart did earlier? Total flop.

I wander over to the colorful display of romance novels, their bright covers with cute couples tugging on my heart-strings, and sigh. Why can't life be like a love story?

2

Step into Christmas

Saturday is my favorite day of the week, and Saturdays in December are really my favorite because the Briggs family cookie bakeathon is in full effect. I walk down the hall as my older brother, Liam, sprints past me in the opposite direction, shoving what appears to be a gingersnap in his mouth. "Going for bagels with the boys," he calls over his shoulder, the front door slamming behind him. Only the sugar trail from the now-eaten cookie left behind on the carpet runner proves he was there at all.

Liam's a freshman at Boston University. Despite all the family time we've spent together over the past year, we still were all super excited to have him home for a month. However, it's been two weeks now, which means the novelty has worn off and he's back to being the annoying brother who leaves his wet towels on the floor in the bathroom after he showers, and who drinks all the milk.

I poke my head into our family room. Our Westie, Dickens, is lying on the radiator ledge below the window in a fuzzy blue dog bed, watching the world go by. He loves to jump onto the couch and scramble onto the ledge—it's his favorite spot. He can guard our house *and* stay warm. I can't resist him—I go over and give his fluffy white head a kiss. Outside it's sunny and bright, and I spot my dog's persistent nemesis—a bushy-tailed, beady-eyed squirrel—climbing up the cherry-blossom tree in our front yard. Luckily for his heart rate, Dickens doesn't see him. "You're still the best watchdog," I say, kissing him on the soft spot between his dark eyes and patting his warm little back. Then I head to the kitchen, the delicious smell of cookies baking making my stomach growl.

"Hi, honey," Mom says, dropping a level cup of flour into a large glass mixing bowl. "You're just in time to start rolling Kringles." This is what we call our holiday sugar cookies. They're my favorite, especially when they're small and the edges get slightly burnt. There are a couple of cookbooks spread out, my mom's laptop is open to a recipe for pecan tassies, and there are even some handwritten recipe cards strewn about, albeit smudged with butter. "Later we'll make spritz."

My younger sister, Karolyn, is arranging metal cookie cutters on our island. She's wearing our red Mrs. Claus apron and large elf slippers, her hair pulled up in a ponytail. I might be a bit extra when it comes to the Christmas spirit, but Kar's a close second. "I was thinking we could do a tray of little stars, then a tray of big stars." She frowns. "Or maybe we should do all little stars."

"Yum," I say, grabbing a PBB off one of the cooling racks. A PBB is a peanut butter blossom: a soft peanut butter base with a Hershey's Kiss pressed in the middle, slightly melted and mostly perfect. My mom has threatened to stop making them because my dad and Liam will eat an entire batch in one weekend. I can't say I blame them. I finish it in two bites and pour myself a cup of coffee.

"People who haven't baked shouldn't get to eat," Karolyn says, giving my hand a little slap.

I poke her back in the ribs. "Mom always says we have to eat breakfast, Kar. This is my morning protein." I shoot Mom an apologetic glance and hold out my phone. "I guess you didn't see my text? Phoebe's picking me up in five minutes. We're going skating."

Ice-skating is fun, but we don't do it often. The rink in our town is used for hockey practice and is open to the public basically never. Phoebe has been pestering us to go skating since the rink opened last month and sent our group chat an urgent text message complete with the siren and SOS emojis.

Mom shakes her head. "Nope, I haven't been looking at my phone. We were kind of counting on you to help, Bails." She looks around our kitchen. "Cookie swap is this Thursday and we are waaaaay behind. Liam already ditched us."

A few years ago, my mom decided to hold a cookie swap

for our neighbors—basically a holiday party where everyone brings a couple dozen of their favorite cookies. But what started out as a simple gathering has mushroomed into a full-blown party with invitations and decorations and appetizers. It is all hands on deck now to make sure the night runs smoothly. Cookie swap is one of my favorite nights of the year. Because cookies, obviously. But also because it's a fun way to get into the holiday spirit.

My shoulders sag. I really do want to help. "Sorry, Mom. I mean, I don't *have* to go. But this afternoon is the only time we could all make it. It's me, Phoebe, Mellie, and Caitlin. They're kind of counting on me being there. Holiday ice doesn't stay around forever." I leave out the part that we only just managed to put a plan together an hour ago. Because really, I knew the cookie swap would come together, but getting my friends together on a Saturday afternoon is all kinds of difficult.

"It's fine, Bails. Go," she tells me, opening the cabinet and taking out more baking soda, baking powder, and a twist-tied bag of confectioner's sugar. "We'll soldier on without you."

Kar slumps down on one of the island stools. "I thought this was supposed to be a family activity," she says, pouting. "Dad's at the gym, Liam's off with his friends, and now you're going skating? Thanks a lot for leaving me with Mom."

"Ha!" Mom comes up behind Kar and kisses the top of her head. Our mom is actually the best and we all know it. She's smart and funny, and she always tries to be there for us, whether it's showing up at Liam's cross-country meets, sewing sequins on Karolyn's dance costumes, or making sure to stock up on the granola I like even if it means an extra shopping trip. She likes the same shows and movies that I do, and she never gets mad if I borrow her boots or spill something on the rug. I actually really like hanging out with her. But not right now.

"I'll frost the Kringles when I get home," I promise, feeling guilty. "Just leave that part for me."

And then I run back to my room to get ready.

• • •

Every time I go ice-skating, I'm reminded of three things:

My ankles are weak.

There's always a long line for hot chocolate.

Kids skate like maniacs.

"This is so fun," Phoebe says. She's a solid skater. She's wearing a skater's skirt and tights while the rest of us are in basic leggings, and her wavy blond hair flows behind her as the four of us make our way around the crowded rink. She can do some fancy tricks. Her arm is linked in mine, and I'm hoping that next to her, I look almost like I know what I'm doing. Phoebe's wearing a white hat with a gigantic fake-fur pom-pom on top, and her cheeks are flushed red from the cold.

Ice-skaters of all ages and abilities surround us, while cheerful holiday music plays. Little kids who look barely old enough to walk hang on to their parents for dear life—but sometimes it's the other way around. A lot of the grown-ups are wearing helmets.

I adjust my slouchy red beanie.

"My ankles are kind of hurting," I admit. Phoebe has her own ice skates, but the rest of us rent them. I'm not sure how the skates are supposed to fit, and the kid who rented them to me wasn't very helpful. I resist the urge to bend down to adjust the laces—I don't want to do anything that puts my standing upright at risk.

"Did you layer your socks?" Caitlin asks as she glides next to me. She pulls off her hat, and her fine strawberry-blond hair is super-staticky. It reminds me of how she looked when she touched the van de Graaff generator at the Franklin Institute on our eighth-grade field trip.

"No," I say, mentally wiggling my toes inside my rented skates.

"Good. That cuts off your circulation," she says briskly. "Okay, now try not to make that face for a second." She holds up her phone and begins taking a bunch of selfies of us. It's tricky, because I'm trying to keep skating forward while looking casual and cute at the same time. Caitlin and I are pretty similar in our skating ability—or lack of it. No way would I risk trying to take photos.

"Let me see," Mellie says, taking Caitlin's phone. "OMG, I legit look like Princess Leia with these things," she says, taking off her brown wool earmuffs. "They aren't even doing anything. My ears are frozen."

A group of boys wearing black hockey skates zips past us, showing off and spraying ice shavings in our faces. Mellie shrieks—she's one glide away from catastrophe. I'm okay if I keep moving in the same direction.

"Are you kidding me?" Mellie yells after the boys. "We're in high school! Have some respect!" We all gradually come to a stop against the wall.

Caitlin rubs her hands together. "I could totally go for a hot chocolate now," she says, trying to get a glimpse of the concession line.

"Is it because Ethan Cooper is over there?" Phoebe asks, lowering her voice to a whisper. Sure enough, I spot Ethan's signature Notre Dame baseball cap and red hair amid the crowd.

"Shhh! What if he reads lips?" Caitlin says, pinching Phoebe's arm hard enough that she yelps and swats her away.

"Whatever. I don't care who's standing over there. I need to pee," Mellie announces, grimacing. "Just thinking about hot chocolate makes me have to go even more."

As Caitlin and Mellie make their way toward the exit, Phoebe turns to me. "Would you mind if I skate off to the back to freestyle for a little while? I don't want to leave you alone, but . . ." She trails off, looking forlorn. I know she's been dying to have some time on the ice to practice jumps and spins. She used to take private lessons, but her dad was furloughed for a few months, so she had to give them up. Luckily, he's working again, but now she just practices on her own.

"Oh, sure," I say. "I'll meet up with you in a few."

"I feel bad," she says, but she's already unlinking her arm from mine. When she skates off, I feel a little unsteady. I keep going around on my long oval loop of the rink, but without my friends here to support me, I feel self-conscious. Maybe I should go find Caitlin and Mellie in the bathroom line. But I hate to do that when the skating session is so short. If you're not careful, you can spend half your time in the concession and restroom lines.

Kids with no fear are zooming past on my left and right. Suddenly I'm moving like a grandma on the ice, inching forward, holding out my arms to keep my balance.

I decide to skate over to the wall. I'm doing pretty well, crossing one skate over the other as I move, aware of the way my weight moves from one leg to another, when the toe of my skate snags a bump in the ice and I trip. My arms windmill forward—and then backward, and I careen back and brace for impact.

But my butt barely skims the ice when strong arms reach under my armpits and pop me back onto my skates.

"Easy now," a voice with the slightest British accent says behind me. It all happens so fast that I'm not even sure *what* happened.

I look up into the face of an angel. A freaking skate god angel. He's tall, with silky blond hair and fair skin that's just slightly flushed from the cold. Or maybe amusement.

I'm not sure.

To my horror, I start laughing. I tend to laugh when I

get nervous or flustered, and right now I'm feeling both of those things in a very intense way.

He's watching me, a slight smile on his lips. "What's so funny?" he asks, taking my arm and gently guiding me over to the wall as if I'm a small child who's wandered off the playground. He's wearing a navy blue wool coat with a scarf around his neck, dark jeans, and black ice skates, the kind that look like hockey skates.

I giggle uncontrollably some more. "Oh, you know," I say, waving my arm around dumbly. "Life." *Stop being so lame!* He is going to think I'm the biggest idiot in the world. Right now *I* think I'm the biggest idiot in the world. "Actually, I . . . I just . . . I was laughing at something my friends said earlier."

Now he looks around. "Friends? Where are they?"

"They went to the bathroom and to get hot chocolate," I tell him, waving my hand in the direction of the concession stand. I feel a flush come up my neck.

"You need to learn how to fall," he tells me before I can formulate any more words. "It's a fine line between falling too far forward and landing on your bum."

"Right," I say, nodding. I reach back and brush some ice off my left butt cheek in what I hope is a nonchalant way.

"And you don't want to flail around. Like a fish."

"No, of course not!" I blurt out, horrified at the mental picture he's painting for me. *Of* me. Is that what I was doing? Why didn't I go with Caitlin and Mellie? Now he's studying me, his hazel eyes focusing intently on mine.

"Why didn't you go with your mates?" he asks, and his adorable British accent makes my knees weak. "Let me guess. You're the rare creature who doesn't like hot chocolate."

Mates. "Oh, no. I wanted to stay on the ice. Get my money's worth," I say, cringing inside at how much I sound like my dad at this moment.

"Fiscally responsible. Quite admirable, really." He leans back, resting his elbows against the white ice-rink wall. "So I didn't catch your name?"

"Bailey."

"I'm Charlie," he says, flashing a dimple at me.

And I just kind of stand there, people whizzing by us.

"Well, it was nice meeting you, Charlie," I say, feeling awkward. "Thanks for saving me."

"Anytime," he tells me. "Everybody falls. Sometimes you just need someone to pick you up." And then he's gone, pushing off from the wall and melting into the crowd.

"Bye! Thanks again," I call after him.

My blood is pumping and I feel a little breathless. The whole encounter felt like something I'd swoon over in one of the romance novels I love—except the chapter ended way too soon. I'm still dreamily gazing in Charlie's direction when I hear a familiar squeal.

"Move! Move! Move!" Mellie cries as she stagger-skates toward me. People do their best to get out of her way as she careens up to the wall, hitting it with a loud thud. Caitlin glides to a stop behind her.

"I thought you said you took lessons," I tell Mellie, giggling as she puts her hands on her hips and bends over, breathing hard.

"That bathroom line was so crazy," Caitlin tells me. "Mellie wanted to sneak into the men's room, but we saw Mr. Richards there, so we couldn't." Mr. Richards is a math teacher at our school.

"Did you guys get hot chocolate?" I ask.

They both nod. "And I burned my tongue because I couldn't wait." Caitlin winces. "They weren't kidding about the steaming part. Now I need ice cream to feel better. Who's in?"

"Me," I say, but as I answer, I'm trying to see if I can spot Charlie in the sea of faces skating past us.

Mellie's looking at me with an intensity she usually reserves for antifeminists. "No offense, Bailey, but . . . you look weird."

"Uh, gee, thanks," I tell her. "I love it when you boost my ego." There's still no sight of him.

Now Caitlin is studying me like a specimen in bio lab. She skates up close so we're almost nose to nose. "No, I get what she means. You look—I don't know—preoccupied and swoony. Like you did after we watched *The Notebook* at your slumber party last year."

My cheeks are already ruddy with the cold, but now I can feel them slowly start to blotch. "You guys are so dumb," I tell them, trying to brush it off. I don't want to tell them about the freaking skate-god angel. Charlie. Because really, there isn't that much to tell.

"What is it? What happened while we were away?" Mellie asks, pouncing. She looks around the rink. "You were talking to someone, weren't you. Who? Tell us!"

Caitlin skates in a circle around us. "Spill the tea."

I let out a sigh. "I almost fell down, this guy skated by and saved me from humiliation, and then he skated away."

"Saved you?" Mellie echoes. "In what way?"

"From embarrassing myself in front of the entire rink," I say, miming an exaggerated fall.

"Where'd he go?" Caitlin asks. She points to what appears to be a fourth grader. "Is that him?" She and Mellie crack up.

I roll my eyes at them. "No idea. I guess back to his friends," I say, shrugging. Despite my covert efforts, I haven't seen him circle past since he skated away. Maybe he went to get some hot chocolate himself. Or maybe he's had enough skating for the day and left.

"I wish we'd seen him," Caitlin says breathlessly.

"Me too," I say. "He was so good-looking. And he even had a British accent."

"No!" Mellie shrieks, shoving me and almost knocking me down. An older couple skating by gives us dirty looks. "You didn't tell us he had *an accent!*" One thing my friends and I always have agreed on is that if a guy has a British accent, he's instantly a zillion times more attractive.

Not that Charlie needs any help in that area.

"I know," I moan, replaying his voice in my mind.

"Tall, handsome, saved you from disaster, and British?" Mellie lets out a low whistle before poking me with a gloved finger. "He sounds too good to be true."

I think back to Charlie's smooth blond hair, his easy smile, the way he dressed, the attentive way he led me over to the wall, concerned for my well-being, his British accent . . .

"You know," I tell her, blowing out my breath and pushing off on my skate blade, "I think maybe he is."

3

Rockin' Around the Christmas Tree

Me: Heyyyy

Mellie: ????

Me: So Sam Gorley told me about a party tonight at Joe Shiffley's house. Any chance you party animals wanna go? 🐱

Caitlin: I have to study. Sorry ☹

Mellie: Going to the Winter Cabaret at the Gideon tonite with the fam. Woooooooooo

Phoebe: A party? Not really into it. We could hang out and watch a movie but I'm kinda tired

Me: How did I know you guys would all turn me down?

I hit backspace and delete the last message before sending it. Then, I text them the expressionless face emoji and flop back on my bed, staring at the Fun Bunch group chat.

The Fun Bunch isn't all that fun tonight. I usually don't go to parties because my friends aren't really into them and who wants to go to a high school party alone? But somehow knowing that there is a party tonight, and that I could be there if I wanted to, makes it weirdly compelling—especially if I consider the alternative. If I stay home tonight, I can pretty much predict what will happen:

a. I'll study. But I don't have a lot of homework this weekend and what I do have I can always do tomorrow.

b. I'll watch a Hallmark Christmas movie with my sister (not a bad way to spend the evening but we did that last weekend. And the weekend before that. So . . .)

c. I'll try to clean my room but will end up making piles of stuff, moving it around, and really getting nowhere.

d. I'll take a nap.

I pick up my phone and text Sam. U still going to that party?

• • •

Joe Shiffley's house is a split-level on a curved block, and judging by how many cars are parked on the street, there are a lot of people here. I drive past the house to make sure it's the right address and park a few houses away. Then I turn off the lights and text Sam.

I'm here! 😀 🎿

I take a quick look at myself in the sun visor mirror. Okay, not bad. I run my fingers through my hair and swipe on some lip gloss, and flip the mirror up fast to make sure no one saw me. I can't deny it: I'm feeling excited. What if I meet a cute guy tonight and we talk or dance . . . or kiss? It could happen. Sam's friends with an entirely different group of people than I am. Maybe my holiday romance is waiting for me behind the wreath-covered door at 317 Willow Tree Lane.

Sam sends me a Snap of her wearing crazy purple sunglasses and a cat sticker that says AWWW YEAH. Then a text: I'm in the basement.

I take a deep, steadying breath and get out of the car. I hate having to walk into the house by myself, but knowing Sam is already inside and waiting for me gives me the courage I need. When I get to the front door, I debate ringing the bell and then decide against it and just walk inside. I can hear music and muffled loud talking, but I don't see any people and I pray that I haven't walked into the wrong house. A woman with dark curly black hair waves to me from the dining room, where she's typing away on her laptop, a coffee mug beside her. "Basement door is straight ahead," she calls out.

"Thanks," I say to the woman, who I assume is Joe's mom, giving her a half-wave.

Dance music is playing downstairs, and it's more crowded than I expected. A couple guys I recognize from school are standing around a foosball table debating something foos-related, and there's a group of people sprawled on a massive sectional in front of a wall-mounted TV playing a video game that looks complicated and violent. A couple of pizza boxes sit on a fancy-looking built-in bar, where Abby Holmes and Lauren Albanese sit on stools, filming themselves doing a goofy dance and laughing. I stand there for what feels like an hour but is probably ten seconds, trying to decide my next move.

Thankfully it's decided for me.

"Bails!" Sam shouts, coming up and giving me a hug. "I didn't think you were gonna come."

"Yeah, I didn't think so either," I say, relieved to see her and thankful that she seems happy to see me. Her hair is in short braided pigtails and she's wearing a low-cut striped top that is definitely cuter than what she wears at school and the bookstore. She even has on eye shadow, which is very un-Samlike. "So, um, which one is Joe?"

Sam points to a guy wearing a black sweatshirt and baggy red shorts, sitting on the couch holding a PlayStation controller.

"Oh," I say, nodding. "Cool."

"Check out the guy in the gray flannel shirt," she says

under her breath, tilting her head toward a kid next to a large speaker that's flashing with strobe lights.

"Isn't that Karl Bartlett?" I ask, squinting at him. He was in my freshman English class. Very quiet, very smart, very into jazz. I'm surprised he's even here.

"Mmmm-hmmm," Sam says. "I wanna go talk to him. Come with me."

We amble over. "Hey, Karl," I say, raising my voice over the music. He smiles back.

"Did you bring that?" Sam asks.

"No, it's Joe's. He asked me to be on aux tonight," Karl says as a deep punchy bass groove thrums out of the speaker.

"Oh, cool!" Sam says. "Show me your playlist."

Karl pulls out his phone and the two of them bend their heads over it. I can't hear what they're saying, but it's not long before Karl's normally pasty white skin is turning pink and Sam keeps snorting and socking him on the arm.

I decide to give them some space. Trying not to draw attention to myself, I drift over to a large pillar and lean against it, watching a group of guys having a sword fight with what appear to be curtain rods. The duelers are laughing like maniacs as—*whack!*—curtain swords slam into each other. One of the duelers is Jacob Marley. He spins around holding the curtain rod, which looks longer than he is tall. Then he leaps onto an ottoman, twirling and thrusting the "sword" back and forth.

"Bruh!" One of the guys, a beefy-looking kid in a Tufts sweatshirt, runs up the basement stairs and then jumps off, sailing through the air with his sword. "You're going to wish you'd never been born," he says to a kid who isn't Jacob. The kid grins back. Then the two of them drop their swords and begin wrestling around on the floor.

I'm observing all this with fascination and horror. This is why I've never hosted a party at my house—people do things they'd never do in their own homes. The thought of having a group of sweaty rude teenage boys rolling around on our carpet, spilling drinks, sliding down banisters, touching my dad's antique train collection—no thank you. Not to mention, my parents would probably kill me.

Jacob can't stop laughing, but he tries to pull it together when Joe Shiffley comes over, looking annoyed. "Idiots, my mom just got those at Pottery Barn. She's gonna freak if you break them."

"Sorry, man," says the Tufts kid, panting. His face is redder than a boiled beet.

"Yeah, sorry," says his opponent, dropping the curtain rod and holding up his hands as if he's being arrested. Jacob just shrugs.

"No harm, no foul," Joe says, fist-bumping Jacob, who suddenly seems to notice for the first time that I'm here. Jacob seems unsure what to do—say hello? Avoid me? Challenge me to a duel?

"Ain't no laws when drinking White Claws," someone yells, holding up a koozie-covered can.

Jacob walks over to me, slightly flushed from battle. "Did you see that?"

"It was hard to miss," I say. "My brother and I used to have lightsaber duels in our kitchen."

"Let me guess—you were the dark side?"

Instead of answering, I cross my arms. "Find your wallet?"

The smile drops off his face. "I told you, that was an innocent mistake. I wasn't trying to waste your time."

Just then, beefy Tufts guy comes running up behind Jacob and tackles him. They fall to the ground and begin rolling around in a manner that I guess is their way of having fun.

Talk about a waste of my time. With a huff, I turn on my heel and walk toward the stairs.

Did I really think I was going to find holiday romance in Joe Shiffley's basement?

My phone buzzes. It's a Snap of Sam and Karl in elf outfits.

They're already using Snapchat filters together? I let out a resigned sigh. I guess it's not impossible to find romance in a cellar . . . but tonight, it is for me.

• • •

It's starting to snow when I leave the party. Big, fluffy flakes fall softly all around me, and I feel a little bit like I'm in *Frozen* as I walk to my car. It's a lot colder than it was when I got here, and I zip up my coat, quickening my pace.

I take out my phone to check the time—almost 10:45—and see a text from my mom: Drive safely! ✳

I like it and shove my phone back in my pocket.

I let the car warm up for a minute and pull out, turning the radio to a channel that plays Christmas music 24/7. The comforting sounds of a classic—"Rockin' Around the Christmas Tree"—fill the air, and naturally, I sing along at the top of my lungs. A lot of people complain about holiday music starting in November. They're sick of turning on the radio or walking into a store only to hear The Waitresses or Mariah Carey or Michael Bublé crooning a holiday classic.

I am not one of those people.

During the year, I listen to pop and country music, and even the occasional rap mix, but when November hits, all I want are Christmas tunes, the more Christmassy the better. I would never admit this to my friends, but sometimes I like to pretend that my life is like a holiday movie.

The snow is coming down hard now, and the wind is kicking up. I put the wipers on full speed. It would normally take me about ten minutes to get home, but it's getting really hard to see and I'm driving super slow. I scoot forward in the seat, my gloved hands gripping the wheel. No one is on the road—I guess everyone else got the memo that it's not a good night to be out driving.

I'm making a left turn onto Big Tree Road when suddenly the back of my car starts to skid. "Shoot!" I yelp, knowing I should stay calm as my heartbeat ramps up. A million thoughts flood my brain. What if I hit somebody?

Or what if somebody hits me? I desperately try to remember what my driving teacher, Mr. Dave, told me. Do I brake? Steer into it? Or give it gas?

I decide to brake and push my boot down on the pedal. But I press too hard and the car slides in the opposite direction. "No, no, no," I beg to the car gods. "Don't want to go that way!"

I flash back to my driving course with Mr. Dave, his unruffled demeanor and monotone voice coming to me just when I need it.

Stay calm. Brake softly and slow down. Gently turn the wheel in the direction you're spinning. Come to a natural stop.

Everything is happening simultaneously at warp speed and slow motion.

I'm on autopilot. Like a robot, I remember and follow Mr. Dave's instructions. Well, everything but the stay calm part. I'm braking, I'm slowing, I'm turning . . . I'm spinning, and then—*whack!*—I'm smashing into a guardrail and skidding to a stop in a snowdrift.

"Ahhh!" I shriek.

In an instant the car is stopped. I'm pretty sure I'm alive. At least—until I get home and my parents see the car.

I sit there, blinking, heart racing, hands shaking. I'm okay, but the guaranteed nice-size dent in my front bumper will make my dad threaten to take away my car keys.

In the distance, there's a car coming toward me, its headlights like soft glowing orbs in the snow. My car is pointed in the right direction, facing the car on the opposite side of the road, but I'm parked far onto the shoulder. The car pulls off the road on the other side of the highway and the driver turns on its blinkers. It's a full-on whiteout now, but I'm pretty sure someone gets out of the car.

Instinctively, I reach out and lock my doors. I've watched too much *Dateline*. You can't be too trusting—even in a blizzard.

A young man is jogging across the road over to my car. He raps on my window. "Bailey! You okay?"

I stare through the fogged-up glass. It's the British guy from the ice rink—Charlie. He's in the same blue coat from before, but the scarf is gone and his coat is unbuttoned, revealing a gray waffle thermal shirt underneath. The tops of his ears are pink.

My heart starts racing again. "Um, yeah, I'm fine." I unbuckle my seat belt and open the door. "I can't believe you're here—what a coincidence."

He smiles at me. "It is, isn't it?" Snow is falling on his head in large, wet flakes. "We've got to stop meeting like this—you on the brink of disaster and all."

He's joking, but it's true: this mysterious stranger has come to my rescue twice in one day. His hair is slightly mussed and I have a crazy urge to run my fingers through it. "I was just coming home from a party when I saw you fishtail," he says. "Very glad you're okay."

"Me too," I tell him, blinking as snowflakes land on my eyelashes. "I was at a party too," I say, wondering whose house he was at. "Joe Shiffley?" I add, wondering if they know each other.

"No, it was this place I volunteer at. Quite a rager," he says in a way that makes me unsure whether he's kidding or not. "How 'bout yours? Quiet evening in or did the cops get called?"

The thought of me being at anything remotely near a party where the police are involved almost makes me laugh. Instead, I shake my head. "Pretty boring, actually. Honestly I should have just stayed home. My dad is going to kill me when he sees the car." I was in a fender bender last year with our old Corolla. Tonight I'm driving our much newer RAV4. Facing my dad isn't going to be pretty.

Charlie walks around to the front of my car and taps soundly on the hood. "Maybe you don't have to tell him," he says, shrugging. "For something like this, I probably wouldn't."

"You don't know my dad," I tell him, shaking my head. A gust of wind makes me shiver. "Nothing gets past him— not even a smudge on a mirror."

He shrugs. "You might want to reconsider. Come take a look."

Afraid of what I'm going to see, I walk to the front of the car and bend down. I let out a gasp. "Huh?" No dent, no scratch, nothing—there's no sign of the accident. "I can't believe it," I say with a gasp, pulling off my glove and running my hand along the wet bumper. "This is so crazy! It made a really loud sound when I hit it." The glow of the headlights creates a bubble around us, and with the snow, it's almost as if we're in a snow globe.

"Guess it's a Christmas miracle," Charlie says, his hazel eyes twinkling at me.

"Uh, yeah. I guess it is," I say, relief bubbling through me. I'd already envisioned my driving privileges being taken away until I was twenty.

"Listen, it's not safe for us to be standing on the side of the road like this," he says as a truck roars past us, sending up a slushy spray of snow. "You're okay to drive, right?"

"Oh, yes, totally," I say, willing it to be true. I'm still in disbelief that there isn't even a scratch on the enamel.

Charlie tucks his chin down, and the cold air that I just breathed out comes whooshing back and lodges in my throat. "So, Bailey?"

I look up at him, blinking the wet snow off my eyelashes. We obviously don't even really know each other, but I have a *feeling* about him. An instinct. I can tell that he's a good person just by the way he carries himself. Suddenly I realize: This is it. This is the meet-cute Christmas movie moment I've been waiting for all my life. "Yes?" I croak as a trickle of mascara slithers down my cheek.

He takes my gloved hands in his. "Promise me you'll get those tires checked out. The treads on the back ones look a little worn, and you want to make sure you're prepared for when it's slippery."

I gape at him, wondering if the cold is affecting my

brain. Are we really having a conversation about tire safety right now? It's like Charlie turned on a switch that says DAD MODE. "Um, yes. Sure. I will."

"Okay, good. Now get home safely before your parents start worrying." He drops my hands, reaches out, and opens my door. Wordlessly I slide behind the wheel and smile weakly as he carefully shuts the door and jogs back to his own car, snow continuing to blow angrily. He gives me a wave and I wave back, then watch as his car disappears into the night.

My heart is still racing, but this time it's because I realize the universe is sending me a signal. The same cute guy, twice in one day?

So what if he's driving away? This *is* the meet-cute moment of my dreams. The moment I love in my favorite books—when the heroine locks eyes with the boy of her destiny. It could be the beginning of my Christmas wish coming true.

It's only when I pull slowly back out onto the road, clumps of snow spitting from under my tires, that I realize we never exchanged numbers.

Unless the third time's the charm . . . I'll never see him again.

4

Deck the Halls

After being dragged out of bed at the crack of dawn Sunday morning to go to church, Karolyn, Liam, and I are back in our kitchen, making Belgian waffles and listening to a Christmas jazz playlist. Ella Fitzgerald's "Sleigh Ride" wafts over us as my sister makes the batter from a mix, I slice the strawberries and warm the maple syrup, and Liam gets the plates and the powdered-sugar shaker—we've done this so many times that we're a fine-tuned brunch machine. Stacks of cookie tins from yesterday's bakeathon line the countertop, and we're under strict orders not to open them. Honestly I wouldn't be surprised if Mom has a trip wire ready to trigger an alarm if we so much as breathe on them.

"Dude, these look good," Liam says, lifting the waffle iron as Karolyn slaps his hand. Because he's home, we have to make three batches instead of our usual two, and he's been known to hog all the syrup, so Karolyn and I try to hide it from him.

"Stop, they won't taste right if you keep lifting the lid," she tells him as I pop a strawberry into my mouth. Karolyn likes her waffles crispy and browned. My brother just likes food.

After we eat, we troop down to the basement like the dutiful children we are. My parents are in the middle of lugging down large plastic bins from the storage shelves. I have to go to work later, but I promised I'd lend a hand for a little while.

"Finally, some help around here," my dad huffs, hands on hips. "These halls won't deck themselves, you know." He's holding a stack of red-lidded storage boxes, which he keeps our holiday lights in. He was downright giddy last year when he found these boxes on sale in January—my dad is very into organizing. His gaze falls on Liam. "Let's get started on these bad boys."

My mom is peering into an old taped-up Stew Leonard's box. "Now, what have we here?" she asks, rummaging through the Bubble Wrap inside. That's one of my favorite things about going through our holiday stuff—you never know what you're going to discover. "Oh, it's my bottlebrush trees," she says, taking out a slender copper tree that's been dipped in glitter. "I love these little guys."

"They're so cute," Karolyn says, holding up a tiny snow-covered tree with a bow on top.

As my dad and Liam march upstairs carrying the light boxes along with two of the giant prelit reindeer we put on our front lawn in a landscape scene, I pick up a large green box with brass handles. Inside are our Santas—wooden ones, plush ones, short ones, fat ones. The Santas go on our fireplace mantel, and each year we get a new one. Last year we got a gnome Santa with a red hat covering his face. My favorite is a Santa wearing a red felt coat and carrying a tiny little corncob pipe. My grandpa gave it to me when I was little. I open the box and there he is, winking at me like an old friend.

Without warning, I feel a lump spring up in my throat. My grandpa died three years ago, and seeing this Santa gives me a rush of emotion, making me feel like he's with us, at least in spirit. Grandpa loved Christmas just as much as I do—maybe even more, if that's possible. One of my favorite memories is of him driving me and Karolyn and Liam around in his Cadillac, looking at the holiday lights, drinking hot chocolate from his big camping thermos and playing Christmas music. His hearing wasn't so great, so he kind of blasted the music, which we all found hilarious. I definitely got my love of Christmas from him.

"Ahhh, an old friend," Mom says, noticing the special Santa in my hands. She comes over and puts her arm around me.

My lower lip starts to wobble. "I miss him," I say, my voice cracking.

"Me too," Karolyn says.

Mom nods, looking sad and content all at once, which doesn't even seem possible, but somehow, on her face, it is. "He sure loved the holidays, didn't he?"

I nod. "He's missed so much, Mom. Liam going away to college, me getting my driver's license, Karolyn's dance competitions . . ."

Mom kisses the top of my head. "He's with you, Bailey. Keep his memory close in your heart."

Karolyn slides an arm around my waist. "And we can make new memories that would make him happy. We can always go blast some Christmas carols," she says, shrugging.

I sniffle-laugh. "You're my little sis. Why are you so smart sometimes?"

She shrugs. "Get it from my mom." And then we all laugh.

"Back to work," Mom says, heading for the basement stairs holding a long pine garland.

I let out a little gasp. "What time is it?" I'm supposed to be at the bookstore at 1:00 p.m. and I'm still in my flannel pj bottoms and a Minnie Mouse T-shirt, with unbrushed teeth and unwashed hair. I push past my mom and scramble upstairs to my room.

Once our house is all decorated—the lights are up outside and the reindeer family is glowing, the Santas are on the mantel and the ornaments are on the tree—I will really feel the spirit of Christmas. But right now, all I feel is the spirit of panic.

As I hurry down our front sidewalk fifteen minutes later, showered, dressed, and with minty-fresh breath, I hear Dad saying, "This should be as easy as one-two-three." I turn around. He's lying on his back, plugging in an extension cord that looks like it would reach the North Pole. Liam is on a ladder sticking up Command hooks and holding up strings of little white lights. He shoots me the look of a trapped animal—a look I sadly can relate to, as it's how we all look when we get stuck as Dad's helper on a project that is guaranteed to last for hours. Predictably, only half the lights light up.

I think of Grandpa, and this time, the memory makes me smile. "You know what, guys? It's beginning to look a lot like Christmas."

...

I'm so caught up in the holiday spirit with my family that I haven't really allowed myself to think about what happened last night. About Charlie. After I'd arrived safely home, I'd fallen asleep daydreaming about him: the way his blond hair falls over his eye in that Jack-from-*Titanic* way, his dimple flex, his prepster peacoat, his thermal shirt that covered what appeared to be seriously ripped abs. His friggin' pink ears. But I also kept tossing and turning over how dumb I was. Why didn't I give him my number? Why didn't he ask me for mine? Whose party was he *really* at? So. Many. Questions!

It was so strange that I ran into him on a snowy highway. Caitlin thought so too—we'd been texting back and forth on my way from the parking lot to the bookstore about my Charlie sighting. Even though she has never had a boyfriend, she is the voice of reason when it comes to most things.

Maybe it's a sign, Caitlin types.

A sign? Do you really think so? 💀 I type back as I walk.

Yeah, you know. Like you guys were meant to be together or something. 🐛 😄

Okay, later. ✌️ I know she's being sarcastic. As much as I wish that were true, the fact that he didn't ask me for my number did not go unnoticed. If a guy likes you, he finds a way to contact you. Maybe *that* is the sign I had missed all along.

• • •

The bookstore is what Bill calls "hopping" today, and Victoria is in her element, hand-selling books, cracking jokes, passing out miniature candy canes to shoppers. Christmas songs are playing on the stereo, and all the staff—including me at the wrapping station—are wearing reindeer antlers and red T-shirts that say SHOP LOCAL. A bookseller named Carol is wearing a red nose and has brought extra noses, but I draw the line at that. The person who was supposed to be my wrapping partner came down with a cold, so it's just been me today.

"This put me in the holiday spirit," a woman says as I tie a green ribbon on the puzzle I just wrapped for her. "I need to get a pair of those," she adds, looking at my antlers.

"Thirteen out of ten would recommend," I say, handing

her the package. "Much more comfortable than the elf ears we considered."

The ribbon we use is made of high-quality paper that looks very sophisticated on the gift bags, but we pay the price: it gives us the worst-ever paper cuts. I'm coming back from a quick trip to the back room, to get a Band-Aid and some Neosporin from the first-aid kit Victoria keeps there, when I stop short, my boots squeaking on the wood floor. Jacob is at the gift-wrap table, holding a large bag of newly purchased books. He's wearing a green University of Vermont winter hat and his usual track pants and sneakers.

"Told you I'd be back," he says when I reclaim my place behind the table. He pushes the bag in my direction. "I made sure to come when I knew you'd be here," he adds.

For a moment I think he must have followed me to work, but then I remember I'd posted the times I'd be gift wrapping on Winslow's social media. "Knowing someone is on hand to wrap might make someone choose to shop here," Victoria had told me.

This *is* very decent of him—sometimes customers browse at Winslow's but order from somewhere else, which makes Victoria a combo of mad and sad. Still, I don't want to show him that I appreciate his returning—it's not like he deserves a prize for doing the right thing. I silently slide the books out of the paper shopping bag. He's purchased every single book we selected together.

"Got 'em all," he says off my glance. "And, yeah, definitely

Dogs in Stockings," he says before I can ask him which paper he'd like.

"You did, uh, pay for these, right?" I ask, raising an eyebrow, even though I know he did.

He dangles a small brown leather wallet in front of my nose. "Yes, ma'am. Used real cash money and everything."

"Just making sure," I say smoothly, pulling the paper across the blade with a practiced flick of the wrist. "Wouldn't want to spend, oh, thirty minutes wrapping all this and then have to unwrap everything."

"If it takes you thirty minutes to wrap, we're not going to have time to go out for hot chocolate," he says, smooth as butter. He grins, amping up the charm that has obviously worked for him in the past.

I smirk. What a player. I decide to ignore this the same way he ignored my obvious annoyance about the other day when he forgot his wallet. I've chalked Jacob up to be the kind of guy to throw out statements like this with nothing to back them up just to get a reaction.

I keep my eyes down and my expression neutral as I wrap, but even so, I can feel him staring at me. "You disappeared last night," he says, sounding both accusatory and surprised. "I looked for you and someone told me you'd left. I thought maybe we could hang out and talk or something."

Jacob Marley wanted to hang out and talk with me at a party? Interesting. But, not interested. My eyes flick up. "Yes, well, with all the rolling around on the carpet that was going on, you seemed a little preoccupied."

If I thought Jacob was going to be self-conscious about this, I was wrong. "Yeah, love my boys," he says, grinning and completely missing my dig. He rotates his right shoulder and then his left. "Definitely need to do some more stretching at the gym this week, though. I felt a little sore this morning."

"Mmmmm." I'm not quite sure what to say, so I become a model of wrapping efficiency—pulling out the paper, folding, creasing, taping, tying. At last Jacob seems to get that I'm not impressed by his mere presence. He just kind of stands there, looking like he isn't sure what to do— probably the same look I had last night at the party. He stuffs his hands in his pockets. "It was snowing so hard last night. You get home okay?"

"Actually, I had a little accident," I admit.

"How little?"

I shrug. "I spun out and hit a guardrail. But amazingly there wasn't any damage to my car. I got stuck in a snowbank and this guy stopped to help me." I pause. "He was so nice."

"Oh. That's cool," Jacob says, nodding. "So, like . . . was the guy an adult?"

"Nope. Around our age. I, uh, know him."

Jacob looks surprised at this. "He goes to Bedford?"

I shake my head, and the bells on my reindeer antlers jingle. Since I don't actually know where Charlie goes to school, I don't feel the need to continue this conversation. I'm also not totally sure that Charlie is still *in* school. He could be in college, for all I know. I mean, he looks like he's sixteen, but he seems, I don't know, older and wiser. Not like the guys in my grade who have duels with curtain rods and smash beer cans on their heads.

When I'm finished wrapping all the books, Jacob sticks a ten-dollar bill in the donation jar for Bedford High.

"That's really generous of you," I say, passing everything back to him. "Hope your family likes the books."

"Me too. And sure, yeah, anything for the arts," he says. He shifts from side to side. "So, uh, how much longer do you have to work?"

"Oh, um . . ." I look at my phone—it's almost 3:00, which means the volunteers for the next shift will be here any minute. "I think you're my last customer."

"I meant what I said before."

I put my phone down on the table. "That you need to stretch at the gym?"

He chuckles. "Yeah, that, but also about hanging out. Want to go to Ben's?"

Ben's is my very favorite coffee shop in Bedford—it's super cozy with rustic wood walls, built-in booths, black-and-white-hex-tile floors, and they serve everything from salads and paninis to the best hot chocolate and lattes I've ever had.

"Or we could get something here, if you want," he says at my hesitation.

By "here" I know he means the bookshop café.

"It's not as good as Ben's," I half whisper in case anyone

from the store hears me being disloyal. And I happen to know that Ben's has a seasonal menu that includes toasted-marshmallow syrup—in other words, heaven in a ceramic mug.

"So is that a yes?" he asks uncertainly, and I hesitate, then nod. It's not like I have plans. And I never turn down a latte.

He nods back. "Cool." He reaches over and flicks my antlers. "And I'm kind of hoping you keep the Rudolph headgear on. It's pretty festive."

I reach under the table and pull out an identical pair of antlers from a cardboard box and hand them over, a smile on my lips. "I'm so glad to hear you feel that way."

5

A Marshmallow World

"Man, you weren't kidding about this. It's amazing," Jacob says after he takes a sip. We both ordered the same thing: a large vanilla latte with two pumps of toasted-marshmallow syrup. Jacob's upper lip has a slight outline of foamy milk, and it's strangely endearing.

I hold my oversized handleless cup with two hands and take a long, slow drink. "Right? Addictive." Ben's is pretty crowded, but luckily we didn't have to wait too long. And we're at one of my favorite tables—a wooden booth next to the window, perfect for people-watching.

Ben's is just a block away from the bookshop, and during the walk over, Jacob and I didn't say much to each other. But once we got inside the restaurant, we both loosened up. The fact that it's busy helped, and our waitress is friendly. It just felt a little strange to be hanging out with him in a social setting.

"Have you been looking at schools?" I ask. This fall,

college has become the go-to subject whenever there's a lull in the conversation.

He nods. "A couple. We spent the week before school visiting big city schools and we spent the days we had off for the Jewish holidays visiting the small schools in the sticks."

"And?"

"Definitely small school, and ideally within a four-hour radius of home." The waitress brings over the chocolate lava cake Jacob had ordered. The cake is on a square white plate with a drizzle of raspberry sauce.

"Two forks?" she asks, holding up utensils.

"Yes," Jacob says at the same time I say "No."

The waitress puts two forks on the table. "Better safe than sorry," she says with a wink before rushing off.

"Oh my gosh, this is sick," Jacob says, taking a humongous forkful. "You need to try it."

"Okay, twist my arm." I pick up the other fork and take a dainty bite. "Um, yum." We polish it off in about three minutes flat.

"So, small school, huh?" This is not what I would have expected from Jacob, but now that I think about it, I can see him liking being a big fish in a small pond. "Interesting. Is Vermont small?" I ask, gesturing to the hat that's now on the bench beside him.

"Not really," he says. "That's the one school I got to see last year. When we were there for a visit, it was about ten degrees out and I got my mom to buy me the hat. I did like it there, though, so who knows? Maybe I'll apply. I guess it depends on how I do on the SAT. I'm taking it in March. A lot of schools I like are test-optional, though."

"Same. I took the ACT in October, but I have to take it again." I like BU, where Liam goes, but I don't want to go to the same school as my older brother—I want to carve my own path at a different school and find the best fit for me. But being in a city seems fun and exciting. A small school doesn't excite me quite as much.

"So you get the same drink every time?" Jacob asks.

I nod.

He laces his fingers together like he's about to dispense some wise advice. "I could have predicted that."

I frown. "Because it's a good drink?"

He shakes his head. "You don't seem like a risk taker, and people tend to repeat their choices if they're happy with them. Less risky than making a new choice."

I consider this. He's not wrong. "With a new choice, you're not sure what you're getting."

He points at me with his fork. "Exactly. And by making the same choice again, you're validating your previous decision."

This is a lot to process over latte. "Do you want to be a psychologist or something?" I ask, wondering if he's going to whip out a Rorschach test or start asking me questions about my childhood.

"Nah, I'm just super interested in how people make decisions. My dad works in marketing and we talk about stuff like this a lot over dinner."

"Hmmm. Cool." It's weird, thinking of Jacob Marley with a family. Kind of like seeing your teacher at the grocery store when you were in second grade and realizing they both existed outside of your classroom and ate food. For me, Jacob is this guy I see occasionally in the halls at school and vaguely know as a fellow classmate. Not someone who talks about marketing principles with his father, clearly chews his cuticles, and demolishes lava cake.

"Now think about holiday shopping," he says. "You've got to admit, it's stressful."

"True . . . but only if you wait until the last minute," I say. "Personally I think it's fun." I point out the window at a couple walking by pushing a stroller. The parents are talking animatedly, with the dad pushing the stroller and the mom holding a couple shopping bags. Behind them is a group of middle-school girls, holding Starbucks cups and their phones, giggling. "See? Everyone is feeling the festive vibe."

Jacob is angling for a better view. "There! See the lady with the frizzy red hair and the black glasses? Does she look like she's feeling the vibe?" I follow his gaze and see the woman in question. She's wearing a wool coat buttoned up to the neck, and she's walking quickly, with what looks like a permanent scowl on her face. She's holding a large shopping bag that she's using like a riot shield to push past people.

"Okay, true, she doesn't look exactly jolly," I admit. "But maybe her shoes hurt. Or she's hungry."

"Or maybe she's just stressed out from the stores and the

crowds and all the faux happiness. Maybe she doesn't know what to buy, or maybe she doesn't have anyone to buy anything for," Jacob says, resting his elbows on the table.

"That's sad," I say, wondering what it would be like to feel that way. "Christmas is my favorite holiday. I've never really thought about what it would be like to feel down at this time of year." *I hope that's not your story, red-haired lady.*

"It sucks," Jacob says, sounding tired. "We had to put my dog down in October, and to be honest, I don't even feel like celebrating Christmas." He shoots me an embarrassed look. "I know it sounds dumb, but Wags was my bud, you know? We got him when I was five. He was always there for me. Knew all my secrets."

I'm not sure what to say. If anything happened to Dickens, I would be beside myself. It really bothered me when my grandpa died and people told me they knew how I felt. Because they didn't. No one knows how anybody feels when it comes to losing someone.

I reach out and give his calloused hand an awkward pat. "It's not dumb. Do you have a picture of him?"

Jacob nods and hands me his phone. On his home screen is a photo of a border collie running toward the camera, tongue hanging out. Pure joy.

"Awwwww," I say, letting out a little gasp. "What a cutie!"

Jacob takes back his phone and studies the photo for a few seconds before sliding it back in his pocket. "Yeah. Wags, man. He was the best."

And something inside me shifts a bit and I realize: I may have misjudged this guy.

• • •

It was one thing to watch the pretty winter wonderland scene from inside the toasty warm café. Once we're outside, it's not quite as cinematic. A harsh wind has picked up. I pull my extra-long blue scarf up toward my chin and zip my coat. Snow has started to fall, a drippy wet snow that makes people pop open umbrellas and pull down their earflaps.

"Man, I hate that," Jacob says, ducking as a guy passes holding an umbrella the size of my kitchen table. The spokes barely miss the green pom-pom on his hat.

I look at him, surprised. "I know, right? That's what hats are for." It's rare that I meet someone who shares my loathing for rain gear in the snow.

He shoots a sidelong glance at me as we walk. "Should have gotten a refill on the latte," he chides. "You look cold."

I am shivering, but I don't regret not getting one to go. I already feel like I have to pee, and I'd never have made it home—my bladder is the size of a cherry tomato.

"Where did you park?" Jacob asks me.

"In the lot over by the diner," I tell him, my teeth starting to chatter.

He lifts his chin in the direction of the bookstore. "That's my truck over there. I'll give you a ride."

Inside the slick white Ford pickup, it's warm and smells

like the little tree air freshener hanging from the mirror. "This is really nice," I say, running my hand down the black leather seats. "It looks almost new!"

Jacob laughs. "It's an old road warrior—a 1972 F100. Belonged to my grandpa. We did a lot to it—headlights, taillights, mirrors, grille, paint, door panels, armrests—everything. Even the bedliner in the back is new."

"Wow," I say, feeling guilty as some slush slides off my boots onto the carpeted floor mat. He's obviously proud of the truck, and I don't blame him. I keep my feet together, trying not to take up too much space. "You drive it to school?"

He eases out of the spot and into traffic. "It's the only reason I get to physics on time—I have to leave at the ass-crack of dawn to find a parking space big enough to fit it."

I've never ridden in a pickup before, and I soon realize how cool trucks really are. People are checking us out and it's fun sitting up in here—it's like our own private sky lounge. There's even a CD player with some folksy-sounding music playing that sounds vaguely familiar.

As we inch down Main Street, drivers are doing crazy things: double-parking, stopping short, texting, and not paying attention when the light turns green. None of it seems to bother Jacob—in fact, he's whistling. He has a strong jaw, a slightly big nose, wide cheekbones, those Alaskan husky blue eyes. I have to admit, he's pretty good-looking. But . . . he also has a fair amount of acne, dresses like a lax bro, and doesn't seem to know about two items called Brush and Comb. And while he's the kind of guy who might give the impression that he's solid boyfriend material, he also seems like a regular teenage boy, prone to bad decisions like sliding down a banister or mooning people out a car window. My mind leaps to all sorts of scenarios Jacob could be involved in, none of them pretty.

Then my mind drifts back to Charlie, who on both occasions I've seen him has looked like he walked out of a J.Crew ad after a stop at the barbershop for a haircut and a shave. I didn't realize how important good grooming was to me, but there's something about Charlie that's cuddly and masculine all at once. You just know he's always going to smell good, have soft skin, and unscuffed shoes. He's also funny and charming—and he gets major points for appearing out of nowhere to rescue me from a snowbank. When I imagine what my prospective future boyfriend could look like, Charlie's face is the one I see.

But it's a face I don't know how to contact.

And he isn't the person I'm sitting close to in a cozy and warm vintage pickup truck.

The ride to my car takes only a few minutes, and even though we've hung out now for a couple hours, I'm finding myself wishing we could hang out just a little bit longer. I'm not actually starting to like Jacob . . . am I?

Suddenly I'm startled by a noise and, to my horror, I recognize it all too well from my dad. A burp.

I laugh uncomfortably as Jacob winces. "Sorry, my bad. That latte caught up with me."

Immediately I come to my senses.

I'm trying to avoid my math homework. *That's* the reason I want to hang out longer.

"Well, thanks," I say quickly, popping my seat belt when he pulls up behind my RAV4. It looks especially shrimpy in comparison to the truck.

"Anytime," Jacob says. He looks like he's about to say something else, maybe even apologize again, but I've already opened the door and jumped out.

If he's anything like my dad, there's another burp coming, and I definitely don't want to be around to hear it.

• • •

In the Briggs household, you can count on a home-cooked meal on Sundays, something that involves more than thirty minutes of prep and takes too long to cook on a weeknight. And if it's in the fall or winter, it's usually something that you crave when you're watching Sunday football.

Because of this, it also means that my family tends to eat Sunday dinners early. Today Mom made meatball Parm heroes on toasted brioche rolls, and there's one waiting for me in our warming drawer, along with a white ramekin of extra sauce on the side for dipping, just like I like it.

Dad and Liam are at Lowe's getting more lights—apparently the decorating has been going on all day and Karolyn tells me I'm lucky I missed it. She's on her laptop in her room doing homework, and my mom is on the phone with her sister, my aunt Amy, going over cookie-swap party logistics and leaving me alone in the kitchen with Dickens.

"Hey, guy," I say as he rolls around on the wooden floor, wagging his tail. I know I'm biased, but he is the cutest dog ever—he looks just like the Westie in the Cesar dog food commercials. People actually stop us when we're out walking him to tell us how adorable he is.

"Did they let you have a meatball?" I ask, giving his floppy ear a gentle tug. Hopefully not, because human food isn't good for him. My mom is notorious for sneaking him treats. I scratch his firm little belly for a minute and then put a couple treats into this green rubber ball he loves and fling it into the family room. He runs after it, his short furry legs skidding on our wood floor.

I'm taking pictures of him doing all the cute dog things he does when a text from a number I don't recognize pings on my phone.

Run into any snowbanks today?

I stare at the screen, my hands suddenly clammy. No. Could it be?

Ummmmm who is this? I type back, holding my breath.

Three little dots appear. Then: Charlie. Then: I hope I have the right number. This is Bailey Briggs, right?

"Yes!" I whisper-giggle, clutching the phone. Yup, it's me! I type, trying to process what's happening. And because I have to know: How did you get my number?

Detective work. ☺

I stare at the phone screen. What does that mean? Has he actually been trying to track me down? Dickens runs back with the ball, his dark eyes bright. "Shhh, good boy, wait," I tell him, holding up a finger, and he obediently drops the ball and sits down. I scoot back and lean against a cabinet.

Before I can reply, another text pops up. Actually you lost your scarf the other night. It blew all the way to my car in that crazy wind. There was a label on it and I took a hunch that it was the same last name as yours

That's weird. I don't remember dropping it, but sure enough, he texts a photo and I recognize the drapey pink scarf immediately, complete with the tiny white label. My hand instinctively touches my neck. I have a vast collection of colorful scarves, all knit for me by my grandmother. Each time she finishes a project, she sews in a tag that says HANDMADE WITH LOVE BY JOY BRIGGS. I must have been in such a Charlie trance last night that I hadn't noticed it slip off.

"Thank you, Grandjo," I say softly, putting the phone to my heart. OMG I can't believe you found it

Another text pings through. It's Caitlin. I shake my head, willing her to stop texting at this pivotal moment of my life.

Charlie's back. So... what's up?

I reach over and pat Dickens's head. Not much. Having a photo sesh with my dog. I send him a picture of Dickens looking at the camera with his head tilted the way all Westies do.

What a cutie

Haha, I could say the same about you, I think, but instead I send back a smiley emoji.

I was driving through town today and I thought I saw you

My heartbeat quickens. I hope he didn't see me with Jacob. Oh yeah?

Mmmmm near Ben's cafe? Walking with a tall guy in a green hat?

Shoot, shoot, shoot. So funny! Yep, that was me and— I hesitate, not sure what to label Jacob. Should I say it's my brother? I feel terrible lying, so I go with the truth—my friend Jacob. I helped him pick out some books for Christmas gifts. I work at Winslow's

Oh, the irony. *Of course* our paths would intersect when I'm walking with Jacob.

That's a great store. Books make great gifts

Then he texts, Speaking of . . . the scarf seems pretty special. Handmade with love and all. I wanted to give it back to you

Thankfully no one but Dickens hears me squeal. Yes! Thank you so much I type, my eyes flicking to my cubby in the mudroom where tons of scarves, all handmade with love, are stuffed into a storage basket. Who knew one would help me see Charlie again? Maybe this is my Christmas miracle.

But my moment of bliss is interrupted by his next text.

Should I drop it off at Winslow's?

No! They might lose it I speed-text back. And then in a moment inspired both by my Christmas wish and every seize-the-day inspirational movie I've ever seen, I type,

We're having our annual holiday cookie swap at my house this Thursday. Briggs family tradition and all. You should come. Also . . . question. What's your last name?

There is also a number of perfectly logical reasons why inviting him is a bad idea and all of them pop into my brain as I wait for him to reply. Liam and Karolyn could embarrass me, not to mention Mom. It might be awkward. We might have nothing to talk about. Our neighbors might ask weird questions. He's dairy- or gluten-free. He is a weirdo who hates cookies. He—

Travers.

And I'd love to

And just like that, the annual Briggs Family Cookie Swap got a whole lot merrier.

6

Rudolph the Red-Nosed Reindeer

Like every year, the last weeks of school before winter break are always a blur, and this week is no exception. School, homework, bookstore shifts, holiday shopping. "Blink and it will be Christmas," my mom calls out as I rush out the door this morning. "Don't forget to stop and smell the poinsettias!"

I haven't heard from Charlie since our text exchange on Sunday, which probably isn't anything to read into . . . but it's Wednesday, and I was secretly hoping that by now we'd be sending each other witty texts and memes and be, well, closer. I haven't been able to find his Insta account, and even if I did, I wouldn't want to send him a request anyway since I don't want to look like I'm trying too hard. I did text him the address to my house and he liked the text, so . . . I guess that will have to do.

"Did Mrs. Edmunds not get the memo that assigning math homework that takes over two frustrating hours to complete each night is not cool, especially when it's a week until winter break?" Caitlin asks, jarring me from my thoughts. She and Mellie and I are sitting at our usual table in the lower-level cafeteria for fifth-period lunch. While Mellie and I chat and eat, Caitlin is flipping manically through a binder stuffed with handouts. "The woman is unreal."

"Maybe that's the point—assigning all the things this week so we can have next week off," I say chirpily. I'm extra cheerful because I love when our school does anything themed, and today is one of my favorite theme days—Ugly Sweater Day. The powers that be at Bedford High came up with it a few years ago as a way to spread holiday cheer no matter what your belief system, and there's a ballot box outside the main office where you can cast your vote for categories like Student with the Ugliest Sweater and Most On-Brand Attire.

Caitlin stabs a piece of romaine and shoves it into her mouth. "Tell that to Mr. White, who assigned us a five-page paper where we're supposed to express ourselves as independent thinkers while discussing the diversity of experience and ideology that characterizes American literature."

Mellie blinks. "That is . . . a lot." She peers into her lunch bag and pulls out a fruit strip. "And so is that." She waves the fruit strip in the direction of the sandwich station, where Jess Jara is waiting in line for her usual egg salad on wheat. She's wearing a long-sleeved minidress in a red Fair

Isle pattern with faux shearling trim with bells. Knee-high black boots and a high genie-style ponytail complete her look.

"I'd kill for that confidence," Caitlin mutters as all the boys in Jess's vicinity stare in awe. Ozzie Mendoza even appears to offer to buy her sandwich, bottled water, and bag of chips.

"Well, it's supposed to be Ugly Sweater Day," I say primly, rolling my eyes. "At least *we* follow the rules." Caitlin's wearing a navy blue sweater with a snowman face, including pom-pom eyes. Mellie's sporting a light-up sweater with a Christmas tree that says GET LIT. And I'm in a white sweater with candy-cane-striped sleeves and sequined candy canes on the front.

Ezra Daly and Tyler Chu stop by our table on the way to throw out their trash. They're seniors and think they know everything. "Ladies," Ezra says, looking down at us with a smug expression. He's wearing a sweater with a rooftop Santa in a questionable position—I don't want to look too closely. Tyler grins beside him—he's wearing a bright green pullover with an actual garland on it. He pulls up his pant leg to reveal a pair of Christmas socks with cat faces on them; they say MEOWY CHRISTMAS.

Caitlin gives them a cursory nod. "Fellow Ugly Sweater wearers."

Tyler leans in. "I'm hoping to get Best Accessories," he says, lifting his chin. "I'm even wearing holiday boxers."

"That's hard-core," Mellie says. "We admire your commitment."

Most everyone at school is wearing an ugly sweater today—and some people have taken it to the next level. Kanbe Lopes has a green reindeer sweater with his own smiling face on it, and Emma Goldberg made a cropped top out of wrapping paper that looks like something off a designer runway. My chemistry teacher, Mr. Hull, even got into the spirit with a sweater showing the periodic table of elements alongside the words OH CHEMISTREE.

"I think we have a contender for Most On-Brand," Caitlin says as Ezra and Tyler mosey off. She points across the caf. My eyes follow her finger and land squarely on Jacob Marley. I push her hand down.

"Mmmm. He's gotten a lot cuter since last year," Mellie says, sipping from her S'well bottle. "In all the right places."

"What?" I say, shooting her a surprised look. Mellie thinks Jacob Marley is cute?

"I don't like, *like* him," she hastens to add. "I'm still hoping Spencer will realize we're meant to be." Spencer Raba transferred to our school a year ago, and Mellie has had a crush on him from the moment she laid eyes on him in her graphic design class. So far they're still "just friends," but Mellie is working on that.

"I mean, I didn't think you liked him," I say, my voice coming out a little sharper than I intended.

"Wait, why so intense about Jacob, Double B?" Caitlin

asks, her eyes narrowing. "Bailey Briggs, is there something you're not telling us?"

I blow out my breath, bracing for the storm that's coming. "Fine. Jacob and I went out for coffee on Sunday after my shift at Winslow's."

"Say what?" Mellie says, her eyes widening. She puts her water bottle down on the table with a loud *thwack*.

"And you're telling us this *now*? Three days *after*?" Caitlin frowns. "Way to keep a secret."

"Yeah, we are your best friends," Mellie says grumpily, as if I don't already know this. "At least, I thought we were."

Both of them are pouting now, making me groan. "See, this is why I didn't want to tell you. It was nothing," I say, rolling my eyes. "Jacob bought some books and asked me if I wanted to hang out. We just got lattes. That's it." I shrug. "And he told me about his dog that died a few months ago. Wags."

"That's sad," Caitlin says.

I nod. "I think . . . I think he just needed someone to talk to, maybe."

"Yeah, okay," Mellie says, a suspicious look on her face. "But listen, if you go out for lattes again, feel free to tell your best friends about it." She points to herself and Caitlin.

I put my hand on my ugly sweater. "I swear on Santa's reindeer."

"But wait, did you see Jacob's sweater?" Caitlin asks. "Very bro." Our heads all swivel in his direction even though I already snuck a peek at him. He's got on a black sweatshirt that says BAH HUMBUG in large block letters. Even if he's kidding—which I don't think he is—I don't like it. I'm a holiday purist. Anything too negative goes against every fiber of my Christmas-loving heart.

Mellie shrugs. "Yeah, he doesn't fit in with your Santa-and-bunch-of-elves lifestyle, but you gotta admit—the boy is hot."

"Hmph," I say, finishing my sandwich. "If you say so."

"Oh, lookie look, he's coming over," Caitlin says.

Mellie gives me a sharp kick under the table.

"Hey, saw you guys checking me out," he says, causing Caitlin and Mellie to laugh and me to freeze. His brown hair is in its usual unkempt state, and he's wearing work boots that add at least an inch to his already tall frame.

"Bah humbug, it's a whole vibe," Caitlin tells him, gesturing to his sweater.

"Speak for yourselves," I say to them, then turn to Jacob. "We're more fa-la-la-la-la over here."

Jacob shrugs. "I wanted to go really ugly, but this was the best I could do. Besides, with my name, it's kind of the obvious choice."

He has a point. It hasn't been lost on me, a walking encyclopedia of Christmas, that his name is the same as Scrooge's business partner in *A Christmas Carol*. I admire Jacob's parents for the bold holiday name choice, which clearly has gone over my friends' heads.

Mellie taps her chin thoughtfully. "Well, what's in bad taste is debatable, for sure."

Jacob glances at me, a slight smile on his lips, and it's making me nervous. He's lingering way too long at our table and I'm getting worried about what he might say. I didn't tell my friends about our "date" at Ben's because I didn't want them teasing me and making stories out of nothing. But now that they know, I'm a little concerned that *he* might bring it up and then I'll really never hear the end of it.

I decide the best plan of action is a quick getaway. So I stuff my trash back in my lunch bag and start to get up from the table.

"Wait, Bailey, did you tell Jacob about the cookie swap?" Caitlin asks sweetly, but there's a devilish glint in her eyes.

"Cookie swap?" I repeat faintly, as if I've never heard of such a thing. My underarms are starting to sweat. What is she doing? I give her my best death glare/fake smile combo. I'm pretty sure Charlie is still going to come, even if he hasn't texted me since he agreed to. How awkward is it going to be if Jacob shows up?

Mellie clasps her hands, oblivious. "Oh, yes, Jacob. It's a lot of fun." She proceeds to tell him all about it as I stand there, wordless as a carnival mime. "You should totally come!" She lowers her voice. "But no Scrooge faces allowed." I shoot a glance at her. Maybe his name hasn't gone over her head after all.

He laughs. "Sounds fun. But I don't think Bailey wants me to."

Caitlin lets out a loud "HA!" and pokes me. "Sure she does. Right, Bailey?"

I swallow. "I mean, sure. If you want to. But you don't have to. Don't let these two losers talk you into it."

"I'm pretty good about not getting talked into things," he says, and there's something about the directness in his voice that makes my heart flutter. The warning bell rings and the four of us walk toward the cafeteria doors. I'm trying to think of a way to undo this, to tell him that I don't think it's a good idea for him to come to the cookie swap, but we're at the door and I don't know how to say it without sounding incredibly rude—or like I'm lying.

"I didn't figure you for a rule breaker," Jacob says as we reach the exit. Caitlin and Mellie speed-walk toward the math wing, which is on the other side of the building. You have to practically be an Olympian to make it there before the second bell rings. My French class is just a few doors away.

I frown, not sure where he's going with this. "I'm . . . not?"

"I mean, it's just, for an ugly sweater . . . you look pretty cute." He gives me a smile and merges into the crowd, leaving me clutching my notebooks and iPad, my brain swimming.

What am I going to do?

7

Christmas Cookies

"Now, don't be intimidated by a cookie. Anyone can make these," my across-the-street neighbor Mrs. Yamano says, tapping the white platter of confectioners'-sugar-dusted linzer cookies she brought. Finally it's Thursday night, and the cookie swap is in full swing. I'm standing next to Mrs. Yamano at our kitchen island, where I've claimed a spot next to the eggnog punch bowl. On my other side is Mrs. Johnson, who lives next door to the Yamanos. She has made a gigantic tin of almond biscotti that tastes like heaven, especially when you dip it in the eggnog. I've learned from experience to pace myself, but it's hard, as everything looks delicious and Christmassy.

"And anyone can eat them," my dad says, plucking a linzer cookie with a perfect center of jam off the dish as he squeezes past us. He's smiling, wearing a crisply pressed red shirt and dark denim jeans, holding a cup of nutmeg-swirled eggnog. You'd never know that three hours ago he was severely unshaven, in frumpy sweats, frantically sweeping off our front steps, taking out the recycling, and getting fires started in the living room and family room fireplaces while my mom raced around fluffing pillows and lighting candles that smell like pine cones.

The day before the cookie swap was a mad dash to get our house looking like the After version of an HGTV home reveal. The floors are mopped and the rugs vacuumed. The bathroom sinks and toilets are scrubbed, all kitchen surfaces are wiped and dusted, and even the inside of the refrigerator has been cleaned in case anyone takes a peek—goodbye, mystery leftovers and random condiments no one ever uses.

Now our kitchen looks, sounds, and smells like Santa's bake shop. There are meringues and pizzelles, key lime bars and Swedish spritz cookies, candy-cane sticks and striped icebox cookies—all kinds of yum. Everyone labeled their cookie platters with their names and the names of their cookies, using small place cards my mom had put out, calling out which treats contain nuts and which ones are gluten-free, and there are holiday treat bags and baker's twine so everyone can bring cookies home.

It seems like our entire neighborhood has shown up. People are so happy to be together this year, and it shows. Every square inch of our kitchen and dining room is covered with holiday serving platters and cake stands, and everywhere you look, people are eating cookies. It's such a cozy scene. I catch Mom's eye as she goes to answer the door and she winks at me. Another Briggs Family Cookie Swap success story.

"Now, how much jam do you use?" Mrs. Johnson asks, nibbling on a snowy white meringue.

Mrs. Yamano taps her chin, thinking. "Mmmm, usually a half teaspoon per cookie. This year I did raspberry, but Keith insists strawberry is better. You just need to let them sit for a few hours after you press them together." She laughs. "That is, if your family doesn't devour them first." The two moms move on to talking about nut flours and the benefits of the toasted or untoasted version of each. My cue to leave.

I'm having fun trying all the different cookies and seeing the happy faces of my family and our friends and neighbors talking and laughing in the way people do when they're caught up in the holiday spirit—but I'm also feeling a little sick to my stomach, and it isn't because I've had too many rum balls.

All I can think about is Charlie and Jacob each showing up—possibly at the same time—and the awkwardness that is sure to follow. After school yesterday, I'd told Caitlin and Mellie that I really wished they hadn't invited Jacob to the swap, but they blew me off, telling me that I was being silly and that I should give Jacob a chance—that it was obvious he liked me. Caitlin went as far as telling me not to be a Grinch. I'm not angry with them—I know they aren't trying to upset me. But they don't know about my inviting Charlie and that's why my stomach is currently curled up in knots.

Some neighbors just walk into our house. Others ring the bell. Each time the chime goes off, I jump.

I don't like keeping things from my closest friends. But I don't want to be embarrassed if Charlie is a no-show. I don't want any more texts from Caitlin joking about how we were meant to be together. It isn't fun to joke about something I'm secretly hoping might happen.

"Have you tried the lemon ricotta cookies? Sooooo good," Mellie says in my ear, coming up behind me. She and Caitlin are both wearing matching reindeer onesies. I have one too—we ordered them online together—but since I am figuratively and literally sweating, I opted out of the onesie and went with my gray pants and a lacy white sweater I bought with my birthday money. Phoebe texted to say she's running late, but that she would be bringing the "Rudolph Spirit" when she arrived.

"Wait, there's *cheese* in those?" Caitlin gasps, wrinkling her nose as if I'd just told her I had farted in gym glass. She stares at the offending dessert. "In a cookie?"

"Yup. Karolyn made them." The cookies are like little lemon cakes—puffy, moist, delicious. "The ricotta is what makes them so good. You have to like lemon, though." Which I do.

"Seriously one of the best cookies I've ever had," Mellie says, patting her tummy. Her eyes flit around the kitchen. "I should find your little sis and tell her." She bites into a mini black-and-white cookie. Tiny bits of icing drift onto the floor. "Is Jacob here? I haven't seen him."

I catch her and Caitlin exchanging knowing smiles. "I haven't seen him either," I say breezily, taking a slow sip of eggnog punch. "It *is* a school night. Maybe he has a lot of homework or cross-country practice or something." *Will Jacob come? Will Charlie? Will I pass out?* I glance down the crowded hallway toward the front door.

"Seriously, these are so good," Liam says, coming over with a plate of cookies and a tall glass of milk. He's wearing a Boston University sweatshirt—red is one of the school's colors, so he's able to represent his school and look festive all at once. He's been hanging with a couple of his friends in the family room watching clips from *The Office*. "This is so fun."

I nod. "One of my favorite holiday traditions."

"Do you think we'll do this when we're older? Like, when we have our own houses and stuff?" my brother asks, a worried edge to his voice.

"Of course!" I assure him. "We can't let a family tradition like this end."

He grins, then reaches over and gives me a tight hug. "Love you."

"Love you too." As Liam heads back to his friends, I make my way around the kitchen, rearranging platters, putting out more napkins, refilling water pitchers. When at last the doorbell rings, I hurry to the front door and fling it open.

It's Jacob. I spy the BAH HUMBUG sweatshirt underneath his coat.

"Hi, Bailey. Merry Christmas," he says, thrusting out a large round silver tray that is covered with a snowflake-patterned cellophane. The tray is filled with the most beautiful iced sugar cookies I've ever seen.

"Wow," I say, gazing down at the tray. "Is that . . . a partridge in a pear tree?" There are candy canes and holiday stockings and snowmen and the aforementioned partridge.

"Uh . . . maybe?" Jacob is looking at the cookies as if he's never seen them before. I realize what's happened here.

"You weren't supposed to buy the cookies," I point out peevishly. "That's the whole point of a cookie swap, you know. Everybody brings cookies that they baked—with care and love."

He shrugs. "Well, I didn't know. There's plenty of care and love here, and for your information, I didn't buy them."

I put my hands on my hips. "Do you expect me to believe that?" I ask, frowning at him.

"Yeah, I do," Jacob says. "I never lie, Bailey."

He's so comfortable in his own skin that it makes me simultaneously impressed and jealous. "You believe in Santa, don't you?" he adds. "Ho ho ho and all that?"

I refuse to dignify this with a response. Instead I sigh and take the tray from him. "Just come in." I show him where to hang his coat, and we head into the kitchen. It feels even more crowded than it was before.

"Hey, Jacob, how are you?" Mr. Millner from down the block shakes his hand. Jacob has barely been here two minutes and already he's run into someone he knows.

"Been seeing you in the paper a lot lately—great stuff this year."

"Aw, thanks, Mr. Millner," Jacob says, grinning. "There was some solid competition out there." The two of them start talking about mile times and hilly versus flat courses. I walk over and try to find room on the island for the tray.

I'm wedging the tray in next to a plate of Pfeffernüsse (say that three times fast) when suddenly Mellie appears out of nowhere. "He came *and* he brought amazing cookies? Ah-mazing!" She reaches to take one but I give her a slap on the wrist, jingling her bangles.

"Can you leave them for a minute? They're so pretty." My eyes are moving at supersonic speed around the party. I say a silent prayer, hoping that Charlie got a cold or is having car trouble or gets lost—so that it's not that he doesn't want to come but that he can't.

Mellie rolls her brown eyes at me. "Call me crazy, but I thought we were supposed to eat the cookies, not stare at them like they're a still-life painting." Then she lets out a long sigh. "I wish I had a boy bringing me cookies."

I snort-laugh. "You kind of did." Back in September, there was this sophomore who developed a massive crush on Mellie. She did not feel the same way about him. He obviously had been checking out her food preferences, because after a few weeks of blatant staring and not-so-casually walking by her locker, he started stopping by our table at lunch and wordlessly handing her a bag of Oreo

Minis, which are her favorite. Finally Mellie had to tell him to stop—and she also went cold turkey on Oreos.

She glares at me. "We agreed to never speak of that again."

I wave my hand around in the air. "Jacob didn't bring *me* cookies, Mel. He's just trying to be a gracious party guest."

Mellie gives me an incredulous look. "He likes you. But whatever." She drops her voice. "Did you hear Cameron Lewis broke up with Kyra Dola?"

My eyebrows shoot up. "Wow, right before Christmas? That's sad."

"What? No, it's not," she says. "It's awesome! They were a total mismatch." She rubs her hands together. "And I know just who would be right for him."

At that moment, Jacob lets out a loud laugh and my attention swivels over to him. He's in the middle of a group of moms, who all are joking and chatting with him. I'm impressed at how easily he gets along with adults—he seems so relaxed.

"And I told him, 'No, Mr. Cooper, we ate the burgers already!'" The moms practically double over with laughter, and one of them reaches over and pinches his cheek. It's clear they all think he's adorable.

My anxiety flares up again at the thought of Charlie showing up. I'd have to tell Jacob that Charlie is the guy who saved me from the snowdrift after the party—and Charlie would likely recognize Jacob as the "tall guy in the green hat." Juggling two boys at the same holiday party feels very out of my depth. Trying to distract myself, I take my phone out from my back pocket. To my surprise, there's a text from Charlie. I didn't even feel my phone buzz. My heart beats faster as I click on it.

> Hey, Bailey. I'm so sorry—I started feeling under the weather tonight, and when I got to your house my head was really killing me. I ended up going to the pharmacy for some headache meds and going home. I really wanted to come. Your house looks great, by the way—I love the reindeer! Another time when I'm not feeling iffy, okay?

I clutch my phone. I feel bad that Charlie's sick. But at the same time, I'm pretty sure he'll get better . . . and a wave of relief floods through me. Knowing that there isn't going to be a circle of cringe with me and Charlie and Jacob definitely lifts a weight off my shoulders.

I text back Oh, no! So sorry you're sick! I hope you feel better soon. Let's hang out another time!

Definitely

It's as if I've been operating under a fuzzy filter during the cookie swap and now that I know there won't be an awkward run-in, the Christmas music is clearer, the cookies sweeter, the mood happier.

I look up to see one of the moms trying to get Jacob to

eat a pizzelle. I beeline over to him. "Hey, remember that thing I wanted to show you?"

"Oh, yeah, that thing," he says, lighting up. He nods bye to the moms. "Phew, I thought I was a goner there," he whispers in my ear. "My cheeks thank you."

"No problem," I tell him. "And I do have something to show you. We, um, have a gingerbread decorating station," I say, pulling him through the crowd. In the corner of our kitchen, where we normally keep our coffeepot and mugs, we'd placed large cookie sheets of gingerbread men with bottles of colored icing, green and red sugars, edible pearls, and sprinkles.

"I think these are the only cookies that aren't homemade," I say, picking up one of the men. *Besides the ones you brought,* I add mentally. There's no reason to start that up again.

"I feel bad for the guy. He's so underdressed," Jacob says, picking up a bottle of green icing and squirting some on the cookie's chest.

I watch, amused, as Jacob decorates the cookie, giving it a green top and a blue bow tie. The tip of his tongue pokes out the side of his mouth, a quirky little habit my brother also has, which I take to be a sign that he's concentrating hard.

"You're like a little kid," I say, laughing as he gives the gingerbread man white eyes and a ridiculously large red smile. His enthusiasm is contagious, and soon we've decorated a little army of gingerbread men. Jacob is laser-focused on his cookies. He's concentrating hard—his tongue still sticking out. Jacob gives the cookie men suspenders and bow ties and Christmas sweaters. He even makes them little sneakers.

"A naked gingerbread man," Jacob says, pointing to the last cookie. He lowers his voice. "It's almost scandalous."

Because it's Jacob's first cookie swap and I'm full of good cheer, not to mention eggnog, I let him decorate it.

. . .

It's after eleven o'clock when the last guests leave. My family is cleaning up the kitchen in that tired but happy way you do after a party you host goes exactly how you want it to. "Let's just get the dishwasher going and get any leftover cookies in tins. The rest can wait until tomorrow," my mom says, blowing out the white votive candles that sit on our island.

"Bailey, did you take Dickens out?" my dad asks, yawning as he puts an empty platter in the sink and squirts some dish soap on it. "And if not, could you?"

"Okay." I almost forgot about him. The temperature has dropped, and I pull his fleecy Christmas sweater over his small but solid little body and clip the leash onto his collar. "Let's go out, D."

The sky is dark, and I watch as a plane flies overhead, leaving a plume of white in its wake. I always wonder about the people on the planes I see—who they are, where they're going. Whether they're looking out the window wondering about the unseen people on the ground below. I stand there, sky gazing, while Dickens sniffs around. He starts trotting down our front walk to the sidewalk, and I slowly walk behind him, holding his leash.

I usually am the one who gets stuck taking Dickens out before bed, but I don't mind. Being outside, looking up at the sky or at my neighborhood, peaceful and quiet, gives me time to process my day and my thoughts. And right now my thoughts are mostly of the Jacob variety. We'd had a lot of laughs tonight—joking around with our neighbors, decorating the gingerbread cookies, taking selfies. He has a good sense of humor, and to my surprise, we have a lot in common—we both are close to our families, we like winter better than summer, our favorite class is English, and our favorite cookie from the party is Mom's spritz.

And Jacob was a big hit with my parents and our friends. I managed to look at him out of the corner of my eye multiple times, and each time he was either socializing, laughing, or eating a cookie. I sent him home with a large tin filled with as many different kinds of cookies as possible.

"What, I don't get one of those bags with a ribbon on it?" he asked when I handed him the tin.

I rolled my eyes. "This holds about four times as many cookies as a treat bag. You're welcome. And don't open it until you get home. Willpower."

"Willpower. Got it," he repeated dutifully. He sent a Snap of himself with the full tin of cookies intact when he got home. Gingerbread dreamin' he texted me.

Despite the fun I had with Jacob, I keep revisiting Charlie in my head. I really hoped that he might be my Christmas wish. I let out a sigh, the sound extra loud in the quiet winter air. I guess it's still possible—he did say he wanted to hang out another time. So I can't be too upset about it. I'd had a good night—and one of the biggest reasons why was because of Jacob. "I'm glad you came tonight, Jacob Marley," I whisper aloud. "I guess things happen for a reason."

Dickens finally finds the right place to do his business. Once he finishes, I scoop up his poop and lead him back up the sidewalk toward my house. Our garbage cans are on the side of the house, and when I lift the lid, I see something on top of the large white garbage bag inside the can.

What on earth? I peer closer. There is a bent, crinkled paper plate of cookies tossed in the trash. I turn on my phone's flashlight and hold the light over the garbage can. The cookies are all crumbled and burnt—they honestly look like they *belong* in the trash. But I don't remember seeing them at the party—and Mom would never throw out cookies that someone had taken the time to bake. Where did they come from?

Dickens tilts his head at me, his tail wagging. I shrug. "Right? I agree with you, D. It's a mystery."

• • •

Later that night, I'm in bed, looking at photos on my phone. There are some great ones of all the cookies—I angled the shots in a way that made our island look about a zillion feet long. I captured some good candids of our neighbors, and Mrs. Yamano took a cute shot of me, Phoebe, Mellie, and Caitlin with our arms around each other. I stop on a selfie of me and Jacob. I took it when we were decorating the gingerbread men, and even though I only took a couple photos, I managed to capture a great shot—I'm looking at the camera, smiling, posed, and Jacob is looking at me, laughing, holding up one of the decorated gingerbread men. It's like Mom always says: cookies bring everyone together.

I'm debating putting the photo of me and Jacob on my Insta story when my phone vibrates. It's Mellie.

So this is interesting

What?

He asked me not to tell you

I frown. Who asked you not to tell me what?

Jacob asked me not to tell you what I'm about to tell you

Then she sends a close-up Snap of her face with a Santa filter on it. She looks like she has a long white beard.

My fingers fly over the phone. What did he ask you not to tell me? Did he break one of Mom's crystal punch cups? Or spill something somewhere?

So get this. We were talking to him when we were outside waiting for Caitlin's mom to pick us up and Caitlin told him how amazing his cookies looked. He got this weird look on his face and explained that he had made cookies and brought them but they came out awful. All burnt and stuff. But he was still going to bring them. But when he got to your house and walked up the front steps, this blond British dude appeared out of nowhere and handed him the perfect cookies.

I gasp. A blond dude? It was Charlie. It had to be!

OMG.

Right? Jacob said the guy was very apologetic and said he wasn't able to come inside but that he didn't want the cookies to go to waste. I guess Jacob ditched his cookies and gave himself an upgrade.

I gasp again. That plate of cookies I found in the trash must be the ones Jacob baked. And there is no doubt in my mind that if Charlie had made cookies, they would be like something you'd see on an Instagram baking account. Everything he did was perfect. But—

I think it's cute that he baked cookies.

He was trying to impress you.

You can't blame him for pretending the fancy cookies were his.

BUT WHO IS THE MYSTERY BLOND COOKIE GUY?

I hesitate, my fingers twitching. Don't know.

Now I'm scared that we ate cookies from a stranger.

I send her a Snap of my face and write I wouldn't worry about it. We send each other a few more Snaps before saying good night and then I plug my phone in the charger and turn it off.

I am 100 percent certain the mystery guy is Charlie. Who else could it be? But why hadn't he told me he was literally on my doorstep? From what he texted earlier, it seemed like he just pulled up in front of my house and then drove off—I didn't realize he walked all the way up my front steps. Did other people see him? Did he talk to anyone? Was he really so sick that he couldn't come inside? And why, of all people, did he pick Jacob to give his cookies to?

I sigh, remembering the sad little plate of cookies I'd found in the trash. Maybe Jacob did need his help. And then my heart skips a little beat. Giving cookies to a stranger in need: now that was the true spirit of the holiday season.

I reach for my phone to text Charlie—my hand hovering over it—and then I change my mind. Instead, I flip my pillow and burrow under the covers, pulling my comforter up to my chin.

What is it you're supposed to dream of at Christmastime? Sugarplums?

I close my eyes. Tonight I am going to dream of boys. And . . . cookies.

• • •

Mom's Spritz Cookies

2 sticks salted butter, room temperature
½ cup granulated sugar
½ tsp. almond extract
½ tsp. vanilla
1 egg yolk
2 cups flour

Preheat oven to 350°F. Cream butter
and sugar together thoroughly. Add
the almond and vanilla extracts, egg
yolk, and flour. Mix with clean hands
and roll into a log for the cookie
press. You can fit about 28 cookies on
an ungreased sheet. Bake for 9 to 10
minutes or until very lightly browned.
Allow to cool on the baking sheet for
5 minutes before transferring to a
wire cooling rack. Enjoy!

8

Sisters

"I thought you said you only need poster board," I complain after school on Friday, frowning as I push the small red shopping cart behind Karolyn. We've been here a half hour already, and so far all we have in our cart is a pair of craft scissors and a roll of double-stick tape. I have to work later tonight at the bookstore, so I'm trying to move it along. Karolyn has a project for her Spanish class that involves cutting out images of food and gluing them on a board and then labeling them. And since I drove to school today and I am the nicest sister ever, here we are at Michaels.

"Yeah, but Mrs. Federico said we could get extra points for presentation, so I want to make my project look as good as possible." My sister pauses in front of a display of silver and gold glitter Sharpies. Anything sparkly catches her eye, even a marker.

"Those look nice," I say, barely glancing at them. "Now where's the poster board?" The store is packed with holiday ribbons, fake potted poinsettias, craft kits, artificial trees, nutcrackers, prelit garlands—not to mention customers. Normally I love shopping here, but the closer we creep to Christmas, the more crowded it becomes.

"Nah, too expensive," Kar says, drifting toward a display of Washi tape and rhinestone stickers. When Mom isn't around to pay, Karolyn turns into Girl on a Budget.

I let out a protracted yawn. I am so tired. I have yawned my way through all my classes today. Our teachers are in the preholiday frame of mind, trying to squeeze in as many quizzes, tests, and projects before we close, as if we won't be back in class in two weeks.

"Kar, come on. I don't have all day. Get. The. Poster. Board."

My sister sticks her tongue out at me. "Remember that time when Mom dragged us to three different stores because you absolutely had to have a black skirt?"

I scowl. "Yes, it was for the band concert dress code, dummy. It wasn't like I *wanted* an itchy polyester knee-length skirt." I ripped it off the moment I got home and shoved it into the far recesses of my closet until I had to pull it out again for the winter concert.

Karolyn picks up a set of nested Christmas-tree cookie cutters with crinkled edges.

"I think we need to get some bigger cookie cutters for next year. We could bake more cookies faster, and a bigger cookie means more icing."

"True." My thoughts float back to last night. I still can't

wrap my head around the fact that Charlie showed up, gave his cookies to Jacob, and disappeared.

As if she can read my mind, my sister brings him up. "So Jacob seems really nice," Kar says, tossing the cookie cutters back into a giant bin. "And he's hot. Do you like him?"

I shrug. "I mean, I don't really know him."

My sister raises a plucked blond eyebrow. "But you invited him to the cookie swap."

"Uh, well, technically . . ."

"You wouldn't invite a guy you didn't like to the cookie swap," she presses, folding her arms across her sweatshirt.

"No. Well . . ." I try to find the right words to explain how I feel about Jacob, but the truth is, I'm not really sure. My first impression of him was that he's a sports bro who likes to goof around, tell crude jokes, and be loud. Now, though, I'm not sure that's entirely fair. Now he's a boy who has been in my kitchen, has had his cheeks pinched by my neighbors, and has given gingerbread men pants and chest buttons.

My sister gives me a mischievous smile. "You don't have to explain, Bailey. It's written all over your face." She holds up a pair of giant googly eyes and waves them in front of me. "Like looking in a mirror, right?"

"*Stop!*" I hiss, feeling my cheeks start to warm. I grab the eyes and hang them back on the metal hook. Then I give her a little shove. She giggles.

I point to the exit. "We are leaving in five minutes whether you find your stupid poster board or not."

"Okay, *Mom.*"

Still laughing, she finally finds the right aisle and pulls out a poster board. "I think I should get two of these just in case."

"Yeah, because we are not coming back here anytime soon," I say, shaking my car keys in her face. "Okay, we've got to go. I have to be at work in an hour."

"Thanks for taking me," she says after we pay and are out the sliding glass doors. "You're the best."

"You're welcome," I say, smiling at her. "And before you even ask me to help you put the presentation together, the answer is no."

Karolyn's face falls. "You're so mean!"

The car doors unlock. "I'm your big sister, Kar. It's my job."

• • •

I'm not always the most organized person when it comes to my backpack or my room or, well, my life, but when it comes to display tables in bookstores? I can't get enough. That's why Victoria lets me be in charge of the round mahogany wood tables where the New Fiction and New for Kids and Teens are displayed. I take way more time than I probably should making book stacks and deciding which covers look good next to each other. Sometimes we have authors come in and sign stock, and those books get gold SIGNED COPY stickers on them. And we sell other things besides books—

candles, handcrafted jewelry, greeting cards, and pottery by local artisans.

I am in the middle of straightening up the New Fiction table—my version of a workout. An added benefit of working in a bookstore: muscles. Books are heavy. After a few weeks of hauling around book tubs, carrying books in my arms from the back room, and climbing up ladders to reach the tippy-top shelves, I definitely noticed definition in my arms where there had been none before.

A familiar British voice from behind me almost makes me drop the armful of thrillers I'm holding. "I was hoping you'd be here."

I spin around. "Oh!" I exclaim with absolutely no sense of chill. It's Charlie. He is wearing gray corduroys with a black sweater and a dark jacket over it. His blond hair is damp, as if he just got out of the shower, and he smells clean and soapy. There is a tiny cut on his chin, probably from shaving. "You . . . you were?"

He nods, resting his elbow on a high stack of paperbacks. "Scout's honor. I wanted to give you this." He reaches over and casually wraps a scarf—my scarf, the one that had blown off the night of my car accident—around my neck. It smells like what I imagined Charlie would smell like.

"Oh! Wow, yes, thank you so much," I say. Is this actually happening? I admit it—I stare at him for about twenty seconds trying to think of something witty to say. I'm surrounded by books with words, but they've all left me. But he doesn't seem fazed. Only Charlie could pull off hanging out in a bookstore, actually leaning on a pile of books like a character in a movie, and make it look cool. Not to mention he hasn't knocked them over. "Are you feeling better?" I ask.

"Loads," he says. "Sorry, that's why I'm here. I want to make it up to you for not coming to your cookie party last night."

"Oh, no," I say, shaking my head in what I hope is an *Are you kidding? That's long in the past now* motion. "Totally not a big deal at all." Then I stop. "I mean, it would have been great if you had come, but don't worry about it. Really." I so badly want to ask him if he's Mystery Blond Cookie Guy. But I can't think of a natural way to lead in to this question.

"You're very sweet."

No one except my grandma has ever said I'm sweet. Now I definitely can't ask about the cookies—I'll go from sweet to dork in a flash. I can feel my pulse start to flutter in my wrist. "That's sweet of *you* to say," I say back. Suddenly I realize I'm still holding a pile of very heavy books. I drop them onto the table with a thud.

"So, Bailey. I mean it—I do want to make it up to you. We're supposed to get a couple inches of snow tonight. That means it will be perfect sledding weather tomorrow." He ducks his chin and looks up at me as a lock of blond hair dips across his eyes. "Would you want to go with me?"

Is the Pope Catholic? I think, reaching my fingertips to the table for balance. "Sure, that sounds like a lot of fun," I tell him, trying to contain myself. Then I suck in a whoosh of air. "Oh no."

"What?" he asks.

My shoulders sink. "I totally forgot. I'm babysitting." For the past year I've had a pretty steady gig babysitting the Parker kids: Adelaide, age five, and Garrett, age seven. The kids are really cute and the Parkers pay really well. Usually I babysit in the evening, but tomorrow Mr. and Mrs. Parker wanted to go Christmas shopping without the kids.

This news doesn't seem to deter him. "Well, can you bring the kids to the park and we can all go sledding?" He smiles. "I bet they'd love it." His teeth are extremely white. I wonder what kind of toothpaste he uses.

I think for a moment. "Um, probably?" In the past I've taken Adelaide and Garrett out for pizza and to the pool in the summer. The Parkers always tell me I'm their favorite babysitter. I'm pretty sure Mrs. Parker would be okay with it. "Where do you want to go?"

"The golf course has some really good hills," he says, shrugging.

I nod. "Everyone goes there. It gets kind of wild with teenagers. For little kids I think Allen Park is better." That's where I always go sledding with my family.

Charlie smiles at me, little sunbeams shooting out of his dimples.

"Smashing. It's a date, then." He leans over and tugs on both ends of the scarf. He's not exactly pulling me closer—but he *almost* is. And I like it.

9

Sleigh Ride

"Again!" Adelaide shrieks with the piercing voice unique to kindergartners as our giant purple saucer skims to a stop, ice crystals spraying our faces. It's a clear, cold Saturday afternoon, and between the sun and the pure-white snow, the brightness is almost blinding.

I grin down at her. Adelaide is wearing blue snow pants, a puffy pink coat, a striped hat, a matching scarf, and pink waterproof gloves that clip to her jacket. She's very cute. "You really want to climb back up the hill just to slide down again?" I ask. But I already know the answer.

"Uh-huh." Adelaide's cheeks are rosy and she has a light dusting of snow on her eyelashes. "Let's do it again, Bailey!"

Charlie and Garrett have barreled to a stop right next to us. Garrett gives Charlie a fist bump. "Dude, that was so cool! Did you guys see how fast we were going? That was awesome!"

We all climb to our feet, our jackets and legs covered with snow. I wasn't sure how it was going to go, but so far, it has been a really fun day. Allen Park is one of the best sledding places in our town, and while it is a bit of a hike up the hill, the slide down is worth it. And the vibe here is fun—whether you want a low-key slide or a wild ride, there is a hill here for you. There are little kids, families, couples—I even saw a dog in a snow tube.

Just as Charlie predicted, we had a nice snowfall overnight, and it isn't too icy or too slushy—it's perfect sledding weather. The Parkers were fine with me taking the kids sledding as long as I made sure everyone dressed properly for the cold. "I hate sledding," Mrs. Parker said to me under her breath. "You're doing us a favor by taking them—plus they'll be extra tired tonight. Parent win!" And I take this obligation seriously. I am not about to be responsible for anyone getting frostbite on my watch.

The truth is, though, I may have gone a little overboard. After I arrived at the Parkers' house, it took us at least thirty minutes to get ready. Sunblock was liberally applied to all visible skin. And there isn't much visible. Each of the kids has on a T-shirt, a long-sleeved shirt, a sweatshirt, and their winter coat, along with hat, scarf, and gloves. Garrett's snow boots fit him, but we discovered Adelaide's were about three sizes too small. Luckily we found an old pair of Garrett's that fit her, and while she wasn't a fan of wearing "Garrett's stinky old boots," I distracted her by telling her we'd have hot chocolate afterward, and pretty soon she was clomping across the kitchen floor in her brother's footwear like a champ.

"You make a cute snowman," Charlie said when we arrived, lugging two giant purple saucers. He was waiting for us at the top of the hill. The park was crowded, but I spotted him right away. He is in black snow pants and a black coat, and he brought an old-fashioned wooden toboggan. "I might just have to call you Frosty."

"Cute snowman" wasn't exactly the look I was going for, but under the circumstances, I decided I'd take it.

"I feel like I can barely walk with all these layers," I admitted. I have on a navy pom-pom hat and scarf. Under my puffy coat, I have two thermal tops and a polar fleece. I don't have snow pants, but I do have on long underwear, a pair of leggings, and sweatpants, which in the past have worked okay. I hate hate hate when my feet are cold, so I have on two pairs of high wool socks and waterproof snow boots. No wonder I'm moving so stiffly.

So far we've been down the hill on the saucers three times. I've gone twice with Adelaide and once with Garrett. "I want to ride with Charlie," Adelaide announces loudly as two kids on lunch trays fall into a tangled heap behind us.

"I already called it. I'm riding with Charlie," Garrett tells her with the authority of an older brother. "We're going to go faster than everyone else."

"That's not fair," Adelaide says, pouting. "You've already gone with Charlie twice. Why do I have to get stuck with Bailey?" Then her eyes grow big. "Sorry, Bailey!"

"Please, don't fight over me, guys," I say, laughing. I honestly can't blame them. While I approach the hill with a little trepidation, waiting for just the right moment to push off, and telling the kids to hold on and keep their arms and legs tucked in, I noticed that Charlie simply gets on the saucer, wraps his arms around whichever kid he's with, and jets off.

Charlie shoots me an apologetic look, then crouches so he's at kid level. "Okay, here's what I think," he says, looking from one kid to the other. "We'll get the toboggan and I'll ride it down with both of you guys. Sound good?"

Garrett is already running back up the hill. "Race you!" he shouts as Adelaide stomps after him.

"You're really good with kids," I tell Charlie as we make our way up. "Do you have siblings?"

Charlie shakes his head. "'Fraid not. I wish I did. How about you?"

"Older brother, younger sister," I tell him. Charlie's so attentive and easy to talk to, and I chatter away about Liam and Karolyn. "I'm the peacekeeper in the family," I finish, taking a breath. "If it wasn't for me, they'd be at each other's throats."

"Vital family role," Charlie says, nodding. "One of my best mates is a middle child. He's the most loyal friend I've ever had. I wish I could see him again."

"Why can't you?" I ask, curious.

"He's, well, he's still in England," Charlie says with a tinge of sadness. "I had to say goodbye when I came here."

He pulls back his sleeve to reveal a small black tattoo of a lion. "He was a bit unwell as a child, and his mum used to call him her lionheart. It means a person who is brave and determined. That really spoke to me, and I got this so I'd never forget to be brave."

"I love that," I say, lightly touching the tattoo. His skin is soft and smooth. "So you grew up in England?" I ask as he pulls his sleeve back down. Each bit of information he shares makes me want to know more.

He nods. "Yorkshire. We moved to the U.S. when I was ten for Dad's job. He works in film production. Now we've been here so long I've lost my accent."

I laugh. "Trust me, you still have it."

"Is that a bad thing?" he asks, looking genuinely concerned.

Only for every other guy in the vicinity. "Definitely not." I'm loving learning more about him and decide to be brave. "I wanted to ask you—are you on Instagram or Snapchat?" I leave off the part about me trying to find him there. "And, um, where do you go to school?"

He shakes his head. "I stay away from those things—I'd waste way too much time if I got on. And yeah, sorry—I go to a private school about an hour from here. Clarence Hall. It's quite small, really."

I've never heard of Clarence Hall, but I don't really know any private schools. And while it's hard to imagine not being on Instagram, he does have a point about wasting time. "Oh. That's cool."

"Well, come on, Charlie Travers. I want to slide!" Garrett complains, tugging on Charlie's leg.

"His mom calls him Garrett Parker when she means business," I whisper under my breath, trying not to laugh.

"Dude, say no more," Charlie says, giving me a wink.

I watch as the three of them pile onto the toboggan and push off. Charlie is in the rear, then Garrett, and then Adelaide. Charlie is holding on to Garrett, and Garrett is holding on to Adelaide. In seconds they are a tiny speck flying down the slope.

When they get back to the top, Charlie motions to the toboggan. "You and me this time, Bailey?"

Finally! "You two stay here, and don't talk to anyone, okay?" I say to the kids. They must be getting tired, because they don't argue.

"They'll be fine. Right, guys?" Charlie asks them. They nod.

"Okay, then," I say, clomping over and sitting in the front of the sled. Charlie climbs on behind me and sits down, his long legs framing mine. I lean back against him and his chin rests against my shoulder.

"Let's go!" he shouts, pushing off. Cold air rushes against my cheeks and tears form in my eyes. We whiz past other sliders, shrieking and whooping. Out of the corner of my eye, I notice a saucer careening toward us, way, way too fast. I would scream but there isn't enough air in my lungs. Charlie jerks hard on the rope and steers us out of the saucer's path in the nick of time.

"Hold on," he says in my ear, wrapping a protective arm around me to keep me from flying off the toboggan as we skid to the left, hitting icy bumps on the hill. I can't catch my breath and I can't talk—all I can do is laugh hysterically. But I'm not scared. I feel completely enveloped and safe. And then as fast as it began, it's over. We skid to an abrupt stop.

Charlie is on his feet, pulling me to mine. We need to get out of the way of the other people coming down the hill.

"Holy smokes, that was fast," I gasp out, wiping the tears from my face. "Those people almost hit us. I think I saw my life pass before my eyes."

Charlie stops short. He closes his eyes and seems to shake something off. Then he opens his eyes and he's himself again. "Seriously thinking we could be in the luge at the Olympics," Charlie says. "We're a good team, Bailey."

"For sure," I tell him. We start making our way up the hill. On the sled is the closest I have physically been to Charlie. Sitting with him on the toboggan, his arm wrapped around me, had felt really nice. But something about the way he said we're "a good team" bothers me. Is he feeling more like a brother than a boyfriend? Like a *teammate*? Is that why he closed his eyes? Is he thinking we'd be better off as friends instead of something more? I decide not to overthink it and just enjoy the moment . . . whatever it was.

I've had such a good time today that I haven't really paid attention to how much energy I've been using. Suddenly a wave of tiredness hits me. My legs are quivery and some snow has fallen down my back, making me shiver. I shield my eyes with my gloved hand. "Is it me or does the top of the hill get a little farther away each time we slide down?"

"I think you're right," Charlie agrees. "Hate it when that happens." Then he motions to the toboggan. "Hop in."

I stop. "Are you serious?"

Charlie does a little bow. "I'm your knight in shining snow gear. At your service, milady."

I don't need to be asked twice. I climb onto the toboggan and hold on to the side. Charlie picks up the rope and begins to stride back up the mountain, pulling me along.

A few people look at us and smile. They probably think Charlie is my boyfriend. After all, it's a very boyfriend thing to do. I decide I'm being silly, questioning whether Charlie thinks we could be a couple. We totally could! Being friends doesn't mean I've been dumped in the friend zone. Friendship is the foundation of every good relationship.

"Are you sure you're okay?" I ask as we make our way uphill. I know Charlie has to be as tired as I am, and pulling me uphill isn't easy.

Or, at least, it shouldn't be. But Charlie barely breaks a sweat as he hauls me up the hill. In fact, he's humming carols.

"I'm having *snow* much fun," he calls over his shoulder. A broad, strong shoulder.

I giggle. "I guess that means I'm just along for the ride."

I wish I had my phone to take a photo of this right now—me, Bailey Briggs, being pulled up a snowy hill by a cute boy—so I could show all my friends. But I left my phone in the car—I didn't want to risk smashing it or losing it.

I sigh, settling back in the sled. I'll just have to remember this moment. Not that I am likely to forget it. I feel giddy, like I've sucked too much helium out of a party balloon. Every time Charlie looks at me, my cheeks warm up. Every time he says something to me, I feel happy. Thankfully I don't see anyone I know here because it would be embarrassing for someone to see me like this. Although, on the other hand, I wouldn't exactly mind if someone from school saw me with someone as attractive as Charlie. It would definitely be a reputation booster.

I mean, who hasn't had a fantasy British boyfriend—and here he is. It's happening to me IRL!

When we reach the top, Adelaide and Garrett are thankfully right where we'd left them. I am about to tell them that it's time to go, when Charlie rests his hands on their shoulders. "Who wants to go again?"

I blink from where I still sit in the toboggan. Is he serious? "We do!" they yell. "Will you pull us up the hill like you did with Bailey?" Adelaide asks.

I am about to tell them no, when Charlie extends his hand and pulls me to my feet. "Only if you promise we can go *really* fast this time."

• • •

By the time we leave, the sun is beginning to set. We're all cold and damp and ready to shed our layers for dry clothes and food. Charlie walks us to the Parkers' SUV—they let me drive it since it has the car seats—and after helping me put the saucers in the back and get the kids buckled up in the car seats, we're saying our goodbyes.

"I had fun today," Charlie says. "Thanks for hanging out with me."

"Thanks for hanging out with us," I say, tilting my head toward the kids. Thankfully the door is shut so they can't hear us. "I'm a little worried that Garrett's going to tell his parents to call you the next time they need a sitter."

"Totally down for that," he says. "I love kids. More than most adults, actually. Kids just want to have fun."

I nod. "I can relate. And thanks for saving my life. That saucer was out of control."

He laughs. "Keeping you safe in all situations—the motto I live by." He puts his hand on the car and leans toward me. "I'm not sure if now's the right time, but there's something I—"

Bang, bang, bang. Garrett is pounding on the window. "My feet are cold," he wails from behind the glass. "Can we go?"

I let out a silent groan.

"Ahhh, another time, Bailey. You heard the man," Charlie says. He gives Garrett a window fist-bump. "Later, gators." Shooting me one last smile, he walks off.

I open the door and slide into my seat, my heart racing.

If the kids hadn't been in the back, I think maybe he would have asked me out. *Thanks a lot, guys*, I think as I pull onto the road, resisting the urge to shoot them a dirty look in the mirror.

"Your phone is ringing," Garrett says as we sit at a red light.

"Yeah, I hear it. That's okay, we can let it go—"

"Hello?"

My eyes race up into the rearview mirror. Garrett has fished into my bag, pulled out my phone, and is now holding it up to his ear. "Garrett," I moan. "It's probably spam—"

He holds up the phone. "Nuh-uh. It's a boy. Jacob."

"What?" I mouth, shaking my head. "I can't talk to him right now," I say, feeling all kinds of flustered.

"She's driving and she can't talk to you," Garrett says into the phone. Then he giggles. "Yeah. My babysitter. Uh-huh."

"Is Jacob your other boyfriend?" Adelaide asks, kicking her legs back and forth.

"No!" I shush her, hoping Jacob hasn't heard that.

Garrett is holding my phone close to his ear like he's a CIA operative getting his next mission. OMG. What is Jacob saying to him? "Tell Jacob I will call him back later," I say firmly. "You need to tell him bye."

But Garrett listens some more. "He wants to know if you are free tomorrow afternoon."

Tell me this isn't happening. That I don't have a second grader as a romantic go-between. "What?"

"He wants to know if—"

I shake my head. "No, I heard you, Garrett." My hands are clutching the steering wheel so hard I think my knuckles might crack. I reach over and turn the heat down. It's suddenly very hot in this car.

"She's free!" Adelaide yells, giggling. "Bailey's free. Bailey's free," she singsongs.

After what seems like an eternity, Garrett ends the call. "He said he'll pick you up at one tomorrow."

"Oh, really?" I ask lightly. I'm not used to having one boy like me . . . and now is it possible that I have two?

Garrett drops the phone back in my bag. "Are all your friends boys?"

I let out a laugh. "No, not all of them." Is that what Jacob is—and Charlie? Friends? Is that what I want them to be?

Charlie and I had a great time today. When we weren't zooming down the hill, we were talking, and I found him so easy to open up to. I told him about my family and my friends, and he seemed really interested in everything I had to say. It doesn't hurt that he's so good-looking, with his gentle eyes, high cheekbones, broad shoulders, and awesome style. And he *did* call it a date.

But then I think about Jacob. If Charlie is the mysterious stranger, Jacob is the boring, regular guy from my school. Yet for a boring guy, we've had pretty good conversations too. Jacob is a lot funnier than I ever expected, and he has a soft side. He isn't as sophisticated or as pretty as Charlie—he's a rough-around-the-edges type of guy. His hair is a little too messy, his nose a bit too big, his laugh louder than I'd like. But he is 100 percent comfortable in his own skin. He makes me smile and I like being with him. And he has a way of looking at me that makes my heart do little flip-flops, whether I want to acknowledge the flips or not.

I'd wanted a boy to kiss under the mistletoe for Christmas. If things keep going well, maybe it will actually happen.

But if I get my wish . . . which boy will it be?

10

Christmas Tree Farm

When Jacob texts from outside my house Sunday afternoon to let me know he's here, I still have no idea where we're going. He was very cryptic when I texted him last night. All he told me was to dress warmly and wear gloves, and that we'd be gone about three hours. He confirmed that we weren't going sledding, skiing, or anything requiring rented equipment, so honestly I was a little stumped.

"There she is," he says as I walk out of my house. He's waiting next to the passenger door of his pickup truck. He has on a pair of rugged-looking khaki pants, a black hooded jacket, and a gray wool beanie. Little pieces of hair peek out from under the hat, which I find oddly appealing. He has a winter lumberjack vibe going on, and I have to admit: I like it.

"Oh. Thanks," I say, suddenly feeling shy as he opens the door for me. I resist the urge to turn around to see if my mom and Karolyn are watching out the window like the dorks they are. Jacob and I are apparently on the same lumberjack wavelength. I'm wearing dark skinny jeans, a flannel, a dark brown fisherman's cable knit sweater that weighs about twenty pounds, and my fur-lined Timberland boots. I want to be warm—but I also like to look cute.

As I slide into the cab of his truck, my phone buzzes. Karolyn has sent me a Snapchat of Jacob holding open the door as I got into the truck, with a heart filter and a caption written over the photo: . . . **Swoooooooooooooooooon.**

I quickly type back hahahahaha and toss my phone into my shoulder bag like it's a radioactive potato.

Sam Hunt is on the radio and warm air is blasting from the vents. "I made us hot tea," Jacob says after he walks around the back and gets in. He gestures to the two large black-lidded cups in the cupholder. "Hope you like Lipton."

"Fancy," I say, bucking my seat belt. At this time of the year, I'm more of a peppermint person, but I have never had a boy make me tea before. I'm not about to complain. It's cold out today, with a harsh wind, but inside Jacob's truck it feels like a cozy hideaway. He even has wool blankets rolled up on the seat. Are we going for a winter picnic?

Jacob puts his hand on my arm. "Wait—before you get too comfortable. Do you want to bring your dog?"

I look back at him in surprise. "Dickens? Are you serious?"

He nods. "I think he'll like where we're going. I would have brought Wags if he was still here."

"I am always okay with adding dogs. Give me a sec." I

112

run back into the house, my boots thudding along the hardwood floor, and scoop Dickens up from his bed. "Want to go for a ride, D?" His eyes light up and his tail starts wagging. I find his leash, a bowl for water, and some poop bags. He's already wearing a sweater with a soft red lining.

"Mom, do you mind if Jacob and I take Dickens?" I shout, not sure where she is. "He says it's a dog-appropriate place," I add.

My mom is more than happy about this. "It's good for him to get some fresh air and it's also nice for someone besides me to take him out," she says, coming up from the basement. She kisses the tip of my nose and then kisses Dickens on the head. "Have fun!"

When I come back out, Jacob is waiting outside my door again. He pats Dickens on the back and holds the door open so I can climb back in the truck.

"Is he a West Highland terrier?" Jacob asks as we start driving.

I nod. "He's a purebred. He comes from a long line of show dogs."

"Impressive. And clearly he's a trendsetter," he says, pointing to Dickens's Christmas sweater.

Dickens puts his fluffy front paws on the windowsill to look out and I wrap my arm around his belly to keep him from sliding. "So, where are we going?" I ask, my curiosity piqued.

"I could tell you but you might just want to be surprised," he says, looking over at me. His upper lip twitches—and where before I might have thought it was some kind of arrogant jock thing, now that we've gotten to know one another a little, it's honestly attractive. "Not many surprises in life anymore, you know. You might want to take advantage of this opportunity."

"Okay, fine." I settle back in my seat and pick up the cup. "So what'd you do this weekend?"

"Went to a basketball game in Clark with some of my friends on Friday night. Did a workout. Yesterday I made some extra money by going out and shoveling snow for people on my block."

"Oh, that's cool," I say, taking a careful sip from the cup. The tea makes me feel instantly toasty. "How'd you do?"

"Sixty bucks. Not bad."

"Funny, that's what I made yesterday babysitting," I tell him. But then I feel a little hitch in my chest and wish I could take the words back. Because right now I don't want to think about my time sledding with Charlie. I'd had a great time but I'm having a good time now, with Jacob. Am I a bad person because I'm having fun with two different boys?

I decide I'm not. I shake off the unwanted feelings of guilt and focus on the here and now. Charlie's twinkling eyes and high cheekbones are yesterday's news.

Today I am going to concentrate on Jacob.

"So you work at the bookstore and you volunteer and you babysit and you get good grades in school," Jacob rattles off, shaking his head bemusedly. "Do you make time for fun?"

"Yes, I make time for fun," I say, feeling defensive. "It's fun when you help someone find the book they're looking for when all they can remember is that it's got a blue cover and it's about a woman who solves a mystery on a cruise ship. And I have fun helping people pick out wrapping paper and making the bows pretty and stuff," I say. I'm on a roll now. "Little kids are really funny—sometimes I'd rather hang out with them than people our age. And if I didn't do well in school, I wouldn't feel like going out and having fun anyway," I finish, taking a gulp of air. "So yep, see? Lots of fun going on."

Jacob gives me a doubtful glance. "I think we have different ideas of fun, Bailey," he says finally, taking a drink of his tea. His words sting a bit . . . maybe because I have a hunch he might be more interesting than I am.

I know I don't have a reputation as being a wild and crazy party girl at school, but maybe what I do have is worse. I don't have a reputation . . . at all. I have a feeling that to guys like Jacob—guys who are friendly and outgoing and athletic and make friends wherever they go—I probably come across as almost, well, boring. I make a mental checklist. I bake, I work in a bookstore, I take care of small children—I sigh. All I need are a couple cats and some knitting needles.

"I'm having fun now," I say in a small voice.

Jacob smiles. "Good. Me too."

"Good," I say back with a firm nod. "Maybe we should switch the channel." I point to the radio dial, trying to change the subject. For the past minute, all that's been coming out of the speakers was a garbled talk show.

Jacob fools around with the knob and "Dominic the Donkey" comes on. "Ahhh, I hate this song," he mutters, reaching back for the dial.

"No!" My hand shoots out and my fingers wrap around his wrist. "No, leave it!"

He gives me an incredulous look. "Don't tell me you actually like this song?" he asks, raising an eyebrow.

I nod. "I like all Christmas songs. Especially ones about little donkeys that help Santa Claus climb the hills of Italy."

Jacob chuckles. "Well, when you put it that way, I guess I have to leave it. I didn't know what it was about. I guess I always turn it off." We listen to the entire song and then "Mele Kalikimaka" comes on. Jacob looks at me and we both burst out laughing. "I suppose you love this one too," he says, rolling his eyes good-naturedly.

"Well, it is Hawaii's way of saying Merry Christmas to us," I tell him, shrugging. "And it is green and bright . . ."

He holds up his hands and then puts them back on the wheel. "Okay. Since you're riding shotgun, you can be in charge of the music."

I rub my gloved hands together. "DJ Bailey in the house."

No matter what Jacob and I do today, I want it to be festive and fun. I can't control where we're going or what we do, but I can make sure the tunes we listen to put us in a happy holiday vibe.

So any song that features Santa or tinsel or peace on Earth? I'm all in. And if it has sleigh bells? Forget it!

We drive along for a while, sipping our tea and listening to the radio. Snowflakes land on the windshield, and the *whoosh, whoosh* of the wipers lulls me into a semi-stupor. We pass the entrance to the highway and head north, driving by gas stations and restaurants and churches. I'm getting even more curious about where we're going. Dickens is curled up in my lap, snoring lightly.

Soon Jacob turns off the main drag and onto a single-lane road that twists and turns. Large houses set far back on their properties dot the wintry landscape, and we pass a couple horse farms. I even spot a few farms and silos. We are definitely in the country. "We're getting closer," Jacob promises as the truck slows down. He sounds excited.

We pass a thicket of gigantic pine trees, their branches weighed down with snow. Jacob points out my window. A painted wooden sign with large red letters on my side of the road says:

MARLEYS' CHRISTMAS TREE FARM

Wait a hot minute. *Marleys'* Christmas Tree Farm? Is that just a coincidence? I hold on to Dickens as we turn in to the lot, the Ford's tires bumping over frozen mud. "A tree farm?" I exclaim, looking at him and then out at the scene in front of me. "This is so cool!" There's a large green barnlike building where groups of people are congregating. Jacob pulls over and parks the truck in a muddy makeshift parking area.

"I thought you'd like it," Jacob says as we get out. I put Dickens on the ground. He shakes his body and begins trotting, sniffing the ground. "This way," Jacob says, heading in the direction of the barn.

"Aren't you working today?" an older man in a blue baseball cap, sweatshirt, and faded jeans yells over to us as he and a boy around our age tie a tree on top of an SUV. The young family who had purchased it looks excited.

"I took this weekend off, Uncle Billy," Jacob calls over.

The man shakes his head and puts his hands on his hips, where a giant ring of keys jingles when he walks. "How you managed to talk your mom into that, I'll never know."

So it isn't a coincidence. "Hold up. You work here . . . and so does your uncle? And your mom? And it's called *Marleys'*?"

Jacob cracks his knuckles and gives me a sidelong grin. "That's a lot of *ands*."

"*And*," I say, "that's a lot of trees." We pause next to the barn, looking down into a picture-perfect winter scene. Snow is falling softly, and people are milling about in winter coats and hats. In the distance are hundreds and hundreds of pine trees. I inhale a deep breath of fresh, piney air. "It's like Christmas on steroids!" I blurt out, grabbing his hand.

Then I freeze. Did I just grab Jacob's hand?

"I'm sorry," I say, shocked. I try to retrieve my hand from Jacob's grasp.

But his bare fingers interlace with my gloved ones. "Don't tell me you're one of those girls who apologizes for things she doesn't need to apologize for."

"I'm not," I say, feeling my face flush. "I just . . . I guess something came over me. I'm . . ."

"Not sorry," Jacob finishes for me, swinging my hand forward. "Because I'm not."

"Oh. Okay," I say, fully aware that I'm blushing. I try to remain nonchalant, as if I always traipse through tree farms holding hands with boys.

"So, to answer what I think you were getting at," Jacob says, "my family has owned this farm for two generations. Hopefully I'll be the third."

I gaze around in wonder. "Your family owns this place? You own a Christmas tree farm?"

"Indeed we do," Jacob says, gesturing to the barn and the land. "My grandfather built it from the ground up, and when it got too much for him, he sold it to my dad and my uncle Billy."

He pulls me toward the green barn and explains how it works. Once you pick out your tree, the workers put the tree in this loud orange contraption that bags the tree in netting. Then the workers carry the tree to your car and strap it to the roof. In the meantime, you pay for your tree inside the barn.

A woman in a blue puffer vest, a quilted pullover, and a striped pom-pom hat is finishing up with some customers. She puts cash inside an old-fashioned cash register, and when she looks up, her face brightens.

"Hi, honey," she says, smiling at Jacob. "This must be Bailey. I'm Christine Marley, Jacob's mom."

Instinctively I drop Jacob's hand. "Oh, wow, hi," I say, both taken aback and excited that she knows who I am. Jacob's mom has his same, easy smile and the same hair color. The main difference is . . . she's much shorter. "And this is Dickens." There's a worn cushioned dog bed behind the register and Dickens goes over to it and lies down.

"Aw, man, I wanted him to explore the farm with us," Jacob says as Dickens wags his tail at him.

"Next time," Mrs. Marley says. "Let him stay here with me. I like having a four-legged companion."

"That sounds great," I say, tossing my end of the leash beside him. "If he starts any trouble, just text Jacob and I'll come back and get him."

"All right, Ma. Do you need me to do anything?" Jacob asks. He puts his palms on the worn wooden counter and lifts himself off the ground, then drops back to his feet.

His mom picks up a travel coffee mug and takes a sip. "You can see if there are any saws left out there on the farm." She shakes her head and gives me a *What can you do?* smile. "Even though we tell people to make sure to bring their saws back, only half of them do." She sighs. "I guess they're just too excited about their trees."

Jacob leans over and kisses his mom on the cheek. "We'll go round 'em up."

"It was nice to meet you, Bailey," his mom says as we leave. "I hope you enjoy yourself."

"Thank you," I tell her as I follow Jacob out of the barn. "I'm sure I will."

We make our way down a worn dirt path toward the trees. "It might look like a postcard, but it gets pretty steep over here," Jacob explains as we walk. "I don't want you to fall."

"Watch out. It's *very* steep," yell two girls who look like they're in middle school as they run past us clutching their phones. "Safety first!" I hear faint laughter as they head up the hill.

"So let me get this straight," I begin, taking in the woodsy fragrance. "You, the guy who wore a Bah Humbug sweater, the guy who turned off 'Dominic the Donkey,' own a Christmas tree farm?"

Jacob shakes his head. "I don't. My family does."

I gesture expansively at the hundreds of trees that dot the wintry landscape. "Semantics." Honestly, I can't think of a better family business to own—other than a bakery. Or a bookstore.

"And I gotta tell you, I kind of think you got the wrong idea about me," Jacob says, with a slight edge to his voice. "The sweater was a joke. Just because I don't walk around barfing candy canes doesn't mean I'm not into Christmas, Bailey. I grew up on a Christmas tree farm," he reminds me. "Maybe you just go a little overboard."

My friends have made fun of my spirit before, but hearing Jacob say it stings a little. I'm silent for a second, processing. "You're right." I shrug. "I guess I'm so into the holiday season that sometimes I go a little hard. It can be rough for me to relate when people aren't as into it as I am."

"No worries. You keep being you. My brother's that way about Disney," Jacob says as we avoid a muddy tractor print. "He's got lists ranking his top favorite rides, he knows whenever there's going to be a new attraction, he has Mickey Mouse sheets . . . he's obsessed."

I gasp. "Me too!"

Jacob chuckles. "Should have known." We wander around for a while. Jacob moves apart some tree branches and shows me how to spot the remnants of a bird's nest. "I think you're really lucky to have this place," I tell him after he points someone in the direction of a Norway spruce. "I admit it—I'm jealous."

"Thanks," he says. "It's fun showing the place off to someone who appreciates it."

"Your mom said something about saws?" I remind him. "What's that about?"

"When people walk through the barn, they're supposed to pick up a saw so they can do the actual sawing," he explains. "And then they're supposed to bring the saw back up to the barn when they're done. But sometimes people forget to bring the saws up and leave them out in the fields."

"That seems kind of dangerous, letting people run

around with saws," I say, glancing warily around for potential hackers.

Jacob laughs. "Handsaws only, no power saws. It's not exactly the chainsaw massacre out here. People aren't just randomly running with saws," he says. "Some farms only let staff do the sawing. But my grandpa says that takes away from the whole experience of picking out your own tree. At Marleys', you pick out your own tree and you handsaw it. And that won't change," Jacob tells me. I get the feeling that he's telling himself as well.

Jacob looks downcast. "This is kind of a strange year for us. It's the first year without my grandpa here full-time, and it's the first year without Wags running around making everyone laugh."

"That sucks."

"Pretty much," he says. "My uncle and my dad said that this year would be our most important yet." He shakes his head. "It's like they have to prove to themselves they can still keep the holiday spirit going without them both around."

"What was he like?" I ask. "Wags," I clarify hastily. "Your grandpa is still alive, right?"

"Oh, yeah. My grandpa's good. He comes by once a week to check on things." Jacob grins. "And Wags, man, he was so cool. He'd run around the trees and bark whenever he found a saw. He loved playing with kids. He loved apples and dried chicken. And he kept everyone company in the barn. He was fourteen when we put him down, but up until the last few weeks, he still acted like a puppy." Jacob looks up at the clouds, like he's blinking back tears, which makes me get a lump in my throat. It's like when someone yawns and you start yawning. I'm that way when I see people crying.

"We don't deserve dogs," I say.

Jacob fist-bumps me. "Truth. My mom and brother want to get another one, but my dad and I aren't ready," Jacob says, sounding like that day is very far away. "We'll see." We come to a stop in front of a cluster of trees and he reaches over and gives one a shake. "These are Douglas firs. They're our most popular type of tree. They hold up pretty good as long as you water them."

"How much are they?" I ask, happy to change the subject.

"We charge eleven dollars per foot," Jacob says.

"Worth it. It's so classic-looking," I say, admiring a tall one with a full shape. "This one is nice." It even has tiny sprouted pine cones.

Jacob pulls off a dark green needle and rubs it between his fingers. "The needles smell really sweet when you crush them," he says.

I lean over and take a sniff. "Mmmm, piney."

We walk a little farther, wandering around the trees. Twigs and pine branches are scattered in the snow. "Over here we have some Fraser firs and Norway spruce," he tells me, and it's fun to see how proud he is. "And our blue spruces are pretty popular too. People like how symmetrical they are and they're really good for holding heavy ornaments."

"Blue spruce . . . that's what we got this year," I say. "My dad picked our tree up at a local garden store. If I'd known that your family owned a tree farm, we totally would have come here to cut it down."

"That's what they all say."

"I mean it," I insist. I point to a short tree. "I claim this one for next year."

"I'll put a Reserved sign on it," Jacob says, pretending to write out an invisible tag and hang it on the tree. "You haven't lived until you've played tree tag. Running through the rows of firs, making sure my uncle doesn't yell at us . . . you up for it?"

"Christmas tree tag?" I blow out my breath. "Remember, I'm the girl who goes overboard, Jacob. How could I not be up for it?"

"Okay, well. First we need to collect the saws so we don't face-plant and get an unexpected trip to the ER." He rubs his hands together. "And then it's game on, Briggs."

11

Underneath the Tree

I can't keep the smile off my face after Jacob drops me off. This has possibly been one of the best days of my life. Okay, maybe that's dramatic, but it definitely is one of the best days I've had in a long time. I still can't get over the fact that Jacob's family *owns* a Christmas tree farm. I imagine Jacob there as a kid, playing hide-and-seek in the woods, running around like Taylor Swift when she was a little girl growing up on a Christmas tree farm. (I have only watched that video, oh, about twenty times.) Toddler Taylor was so cute. Toddler Jacob would have been pretty darn adorable. When we were leaving the farm, Jacob took Dickens on a run through the trees. Dickens was panting, his little pink tongue hanging out of his mouth, and Jacob was egging him on to go faster as I laughed.

So basically? He's adorable now.

I've tried to fight how I'm feeling, but it's no use. Jacob makes me happy. He's sweet to his mom. He's hardworking.

He's straightforward. And he has a soft spot for dogs. All the traits I've projected on him at school . . . some of them might have been accurate, but not all of them. I realize it isn't fair to judge a person until you get to know them. And I am liking getting to know him.

My dad and Liam are watching Sunday Night Football and are so busy yelling at the TV that they don't even notice me walk in holding Dickens. "I feel so seen," I say to their backs as I enter the kitchen, where I lower him to the floor. Then I warm up a bowl of spaghetti Mom has left for me. This is the second Sunday dinner I've missed in a row, and by the way the kitchen smells, I have a pretty good hunch there was garlic bread and Liam ate it all.

"Here you go, D," I say to Dickens, filling his bowl with kibble. He wags his tail. I shake some Parmesan cheese onto my pasta and then shake some more on top of his kibble before putting his bowl down next to his water. "Eat up, dude."

I pour myself a glass of water and sit at the island. This had been a day. Jacob really opened up to me. It makes me feel special knowing that he considers me someone he can confide in. Though I'm not sure I should put too much weight on it, I decide, absently twirling my pasta. It's hard to imagine any of the guys he was dueling with at the party or hanging out with at school being sympathetic about losing your dog. I have a hunch he keeps things on a bro level with them. I've seen it with my own brother: guys have deep, real feelings . . . but they don't always show them.

Not that Jacob's friends would be mean about it or

anything. In fact, if he had posted about his dog's passing on Instagram—which I know he didn't, because I went back through his feed for the past year—people would have left all kinds of sympathetic comments, like *So sorry for your loss* and *Love you, man* and *Here for you, bro.* But it would just be a bunch of words and likes—it was a lot different to have a face-to-face conversation or to sit and really listen.

I pull out my phone and reply to a few texts and Snap-chats from my friends while I eat. Then I put my dishes in the dishwasher and go up to my room. I still have home-work to do, and I want to shower before Karolyn takes over the bathroom. She has a very intense regimen on Sunday nights—she washes her hair, applies a fruit-scented condi-tioning mask, waits for thirty minutes, then rinses it off, all while hogging the bathroom. She insists that since it's only a once-a-week thing, I can deal.

It feels good to peel off all the layers and wiggle my toes after a day spent outside and in boots. After I shower, I put on a pair of flannel pj bottoms and a T-shirt, wrap my hair up in my Turbie Twist, and slather peppermint body lo-tion on my legs. I have a bunch of beauty products I only use during the holidays—candy-cane body scrubs, marsh-mallow lip balms. I even have a body spray called Winter Wilderness. It's a bit extra, but I apply it anyway.

An hour later, I've finished all my homework and am lying on my bed scrolling through Instagram on my phone and listening to music when there's a knock at my door.

"Laundry fairy!" Mom pushes open the door, a stack of folded tops and lacy underwear in her hands. She puts it on top of my dresser and inhales. "It smells like a peppermint explosion in here."

I shrug. "What can I say? I like to moisturize."

She sits down on the edge of my bed. I know what's coming. "So, by the way you're acting it seems like you had a pretty good time today," she says, her tone light.

"How am I acting?" I ask, trying to stay poker-faced. Then my lips split into a grin. "Yeah. I did have a pretty good time."

My mom smiles back at me. "Do you want to tell me about it?"

And so I do. I tell her everything, from the Christmas tunes in the truck to the fact that Jacob made us tea to the bigger fact that his family owns a tree farm. I tell her about Jacob's mom and how the two of them have the exact same smile and how everyone was so nice to me.

"Well I'd hope so," she says, nudging my shoulder. "You're a real catch."

"Mom, stop." I lean back on my plush cream-colored high-backed reading pillow. "Don't say things like that if you want me to keep talking."

She laughs. "Knowing you, I can't believe you didn't come home with a tree."

I hesitate. "I . . . did?" I say, giving her my best *I know you really love me so please don't kill me* look. "Jacob's family insisted that I leave with a tree," I add quickly. "I didn't want to hurt their feelings."

Mom looks around my bedroom with a confused expression, as if the tree were going to pop out of my closet. "Uh, okay," she says. "But where is it?"

"On the front porch," I say. "It's really small. We named it Wilbur."

"The runt of the pine trees, huh?" Mom says, recognizing the *Charlotte's Web* reference like I knew she would.

"Yep." I roll onto my side. "I didn't want to bring it in until we figured out where it can go."

"How about right here, in your room?" Mom asks. "We can put it next to your dresser." She raises an eyebrow as she takes in the piles of clutter next to my bed. "That is, if it will fit."

"Oh, it'll fit," I say excitedly. "I love that idea."

Mom kicks off her slippers and lies down facing me, propping herself up on one arm. "But do you *love* Jacob?" she asks, using what I guess she thinks is a French accent. Instead she sounds like she has a bad cold.

"If you want me to tell you things, can you not?" I say with a frown. Of the three of us, I am the one sibling my parents can count on to tell them every minute detail of their day, but right now I'm not in the mood. I wave my finger at her. "That was a really dumb thing to say."

She holds up the hand she isn't using to support herself. "I'm kidding, Bailey. *Obviously*." Then she winks. "But Jacob did look pretty happy to see you, from what I could tell. And I liked that he held the door for you."

"Argh! I knew you guys were watching us out the window," I groan, whacking her on the thigh with my furry avocado pillow.

But the weird accent she used makes me think of accents, and then I think about Charlie. Cute, witty, model-perfect Charlie. He hasn't entered my mind the entire day. It's like my head only has room for one guy at a time. When I'm with Jacob, he's all I can think of. And when I'm with Charlie? Same. Thinking of him now makes me feel confused, and almost sick to my stomach. I don't want to hurt either of them.

"Jacob seems like a fun person to spend time with, and he's a gentleman," Mom muses, picking a long stray hair off my quilt and tossing it into the trash can next to my bed.

It's strange to hear her say this because (1) I highly value my mom's opinion and she is usually right about people, and (2) I never thought Jacob would be placed in the "gentleman" category.

"Yeah, a gentleman," I echo, but now I'm the one who sounds weird. "Mom, do you think you can like two boys at once?" I blurt out the question that has been plaguing me. "Hypothetically speaking."

"Like, *like* them?" she asks.

I nod, nibbling on my lip. "And please don't ask me any questions."

"Sure," she says simply. "You can even like three people. Or four." She chuckles. "Remember that crazy last season of *The Bachelor?*"

I grimace. "Don't remind me. Also, let's not get carried away here."

"Well, in all seriousness, of course you can like more than one person," Mom says firmly. "There are a lot of smart, funny, cool people in the world. And at your age, you don't have to limit yourself to just one. When you're in high school, it's like a boy buffet. All you have to do is grab a plate."

I smirk. "But what if your eyes are bigger than your plate?" I say, remembering the Winnie-the-Pooh breakfast buffet we did a few years ago at Disney World where Liam piled so much food on his dish, Tigger covered his eyes in disbelief. "And . . . if you're holding two plates, you have to put one of them down eventually," I say, playing along with Mom's analogy.

"True," Mom agrees, looking thoughtful. "But until you're ready to eat, you can hold those plates for as long as you want to."

I reach over to my laptop and turn up the Kelly Clarkson Christmas song that's playing in a not-so-subtle signal that I want no more talk of buffets. "I suppose."

Mom touches my cheek. "I don't suppose you want to tell me about this other boy."

"Nope," I say, scrunching my nose. "Besides, remember? It was hypothetically speaking."

Mom taps her chin. "Ahhh, yes, that's right. It's always good to have a couple of hypothetical boys waiting in the wings. Wing men. Or . . . wing boys."

"Not funny." I stretch my arms. "I'm pretty tired." I tilt my head toward the door. "Good night, Mom."

"Am I being kicked out?" Mom asks, getting up. "Fine, I can take a hint." She kisses my head and makes to leave. "But wait, honey," she says, hesitating in my doorway. "I meant to ask you. The other day you mentioned something about a gift exchange with the girls. What's going on with that?"

"Yeah, me and Phoebe and Mellie and Caitlin all drew names. I got Phoebe."

"Oh, she'll be fun to shop for," Mom says, her face brightening. "You could get her cute socks or gloves or a coffee mug filled with candy. I saw some nice ones at the Bee and Bonnet."

"Mmmmm, those all sound good," I say, yawning exaggeratedly. Last year my friends and I all exchanged holiday gifts, but it got a little expensive, so this year, we decided to draw names and not tell each other who we have. We set a limit of fifteen dollars, which seems like a decent enough budget. "We're doing it on Thursday, so I have to go out one night this week and shop."

Mom nods. "Okay. You can probably find something downtown, but if you want me to take you to the mall, that might be fun. I have some last-minute gifts to pick up. I like to have a few extra things on hand and surprise people who aren't expecting a gift. We could make a night of it."

"Maybe," I say, yawning again. I put my laptop on my nightstand and plug in the charger. "Okay, Mom. I need to go to sleep."

"Say no more." She blows me a kiss. "Sweet dreams, honey."

"Sweet dreams."

After Mom leaves, I take off the Turbie Twist and shake my hair out. It's still pretty damp, but I like to give myself a break from blow-drying. I slide under the flannel covers and pull the comforter up to my chin.

I do some of my best thinking in the minutes before I fall asleep and tonight is no exception. Lying there, thinking about the day, I have an idea. I'm Phoebe's Secret Santa, but there's no reason I can't be Jacob's Secret Santa too. Nothing expensive or overly personal—just something that makes him feel the yuletide spirit. My mom's plan to pick up some extra gifts sparked an idea. Maybe if he gets a surprise gift, it will remind him just how magical the holiday season really is. It's the time of year when you can look back on the year you had—the good moments and the bad ones—and look ahead to a new year filled with fresh possibilities. I know it isn't a guarantee, but maybe the right gift can help bring back his Christmas spirit.

Because after our day together at Marleys' Christmas Tree Farm, it's clear that Jacob once had a lot of holiday spirit.

And if anyone can help him get it back, it's me.

"Hey," he calls over to us, grinning. "Briggs."

"Oh, hi," I say, giving him a little wave like a dork. I slow down for a second, wondering if he wants to talk, but he's already gone. I look over my shoulder and see him joking around with Darius Baker, who is already over six feet tall and looks like he weighs as much as Jacob and me combined.

I whip my head back around, hoping no one had seen my eyes following him. Of course Mellie had.

"That is what I'm talking about," Mellie says as we head into the stairwell. It's hard to hear her in the echoey space. People jostle for room, bumping into us with their books and elbows.

"What?" I say. My heartbeat has quickened, and I take a slow, deep breath, willing it to go back to my normal rate.

"What *are* you and Jacob?" she demands as we reach the first floor. Normally this is where we split off. Mellie has anthropology and I have Foundations of Art. We move over to the side next to a bank of lockers.

"What do you mean, what *are* we?" I ask, pretending I don't know what she means.

Mellie gives me the same look she gives Phoebe when she refuses to use a straw because turtles but buys a plastic water bottle. "You like him, he likes you—so are you guys dating or what?"

I have been wondering this myself. "I mean—I'm not sure, exactly. We had a great time yesterday. . . ." I trail off, my voice dropping. I texted my friends in our group chat about the Christmas tree farm with Jacob. I didn't tell them

12

Blue Christmas

"So," Mr. Cloverhill says, his hands clasped behind his back. He strolls down the aisles of the classroom, his thick black-rimmed glasses sliding down his nose. "What are some examples from the story that give it a dreamlike feel?" It's third period English class on Monday morning and we are discussing Nathaniel Hawthorne's "Young Goodman Brown." It's about this guy who heads off into the woods while his wife stays at home worrying about him. He meets up with all these different characters who test him and expose his true nature.

We are in the middle of a unit on Dark Romanticism, and most of my class is pretty into it. Basically, the Dark Romantic writers lived up to their name. They wrote about the creepy and dark side of nature and how anyone can be evil. So far we have read a bunch of Edgar Allan Poe poetry, some Emily Dickinson poems, and *The House of the Seven Gables*.

Yara Allen raises her hand. "When Faith says, 'A lone woman is troubled with such dreams and such thoughts that she's afeared of herself sometimes. Pray tarry with me this night, dear husband, of all nights in the year.'"

I can relate. Last night I had tossed and turned, dreaming one strange dream after the other. In the morning I couldn't remember any of them clearly, but I felt unsettled—and sleepy. I blink a few times and sit up straighter in my plastic chair. Mr. Cloverhill likes to call unexpectedly on people. I have to be awake.

"I like where you're going with this," the teacher tells Yara. "Anyone else?"

"When the narrator asks, 'Had Goodman Brown fallen asleep in the forest and only dreamed a wild dream of a witch-meeting?'" Min Park says.

Evan Gibson crosses his arms, his long legs sticking out from the front of his tiny desk. "But like, how are we supposed to know what part's a dream and what part's real?"

Our teacher points at him. "Bingo. But even if it was a dream, Goodman Brown realizes that he can't forget what the dream told him."

Mellie raises her hand. "Yeah, it's like he can't unsee it. Every time he looks at his neighbors, he's going to always wonder about them."

Mr. Cloverhill chatters on about allegories and the Dark Romantics until the bell rings.

Mellie and I head out together. "I didn't finish the char-

acter analysis chart," she says as we walk down the crowded hallway. "Can I see yours?"

"Yeah, I'll send it to you."

"Thanks." She lifts her chin toward Kaylee Zimmer, who is filling her water bottle at the filling station. Kaylee is not our favorite—she picked on Caitlin back in middle school and we've never forgotten it. Kaylee is busy looking at her phone, her mouth hanging open as always. She doesn't notice that the water bottle is overflowing onto her shoes. "What a dummy," Mellie mutters under her breath as Kaylee jumps back from the fountain with a yelp, spilling even more water on herself.

"Don't you get the feeling that everyone was smarter back in Hawthorne's time?" Mellie says. "Today we have to deal with people like her."

I nod. Sometimes I just want to read things for fun and not analyze everything. It kind of sucks the joy out of reading. "Why does everything have to be a symbol?" I ask as we dodge a freshman with an instrument case. Though I do like Mr. Cloverhill. He is always so enthusiastic about whatever we are reading, and he never does things like have pop quizzes or call on you when you are obviously trying to hide.

Mellie sighs. "I wish people would just say what they're thinking. It would make life a whole lot easier."

Suddenly I see Jacob across the hall. It totally catches me off guard, because I've never seen him in this wing of the school after third period.

everything—but I guess I told them enough to make Mellie jump to conclusions.

"So you're dating, then." Mellie says it as a statement.

I do a wishy-washy shrug. "I wouldn't say that." While my friends know about Jacob, they still don't know that much about Charlie. He exists outside the walls of Bedford High, and I like it that way. I feel unusually protective about our time together—it's almost like if I tell people about him, they'll ask lots of questions that I can't answer—like where he lives or if he'll ask me out—and it will start to feel less real.

And I want it to feel real.

I am like Young Goodman Brown. What is a dream? What is real?

Maybe analyzing things *is* the way to learn the truth.

"You need to DTR this thing, Bailey," Mellie says emphatically as she sends off a text.

"Huh?" I ask, startled. "What are you talking about?"

"Um, can I get in here?" a girl in a sherpa jacket asks, pointing to one of the lockers. She is holding a gigantic yellow binder with half the papers falling out of it.

We scoot down a few feet.

"DTR: Define the Relationship." Mellie rattles off the words like she's a life coach instead of a high school junior. "You have to ask him what you two are. Like, if you're a couple or not."

"I'm not doing that," I protest, grimacing. "That's a terrible idea."

Mellie shakes her head as if I'm the weirdo. "Get with the program, Bailey. My mom said it's a must." Mellie's mom is her go-to on relationships. Her parents got divorced when we were in fourth grade. Her dad ended up getting married to someone else, but her mom, Deirdre, has embraced the single life. She uses a bunch of dating apps, she teaches Zumba at the Y, and she always seems to be going out on a date. Deirdre dresses very stylishly, wears statement jewelry, and has hair longer than any mom I know. I've never seen her without her nails done.

"My mom wasted a lot of time on different guys after she and my dad split up," Mellie says. "You have no idea how many losers are out there. Now she's really up-front about what she wants in a relationship. Once she has a few dates with someone, if she likes them, she asks them point-blank where things stand."

I frown. "But she's an adult, Mellie. She doesn't want to waste time on some guy who doesn't like her as much as she likes him."

The girl with the yellow binder is lingering at her locker, and I have a feeling she's eavesdropping on us. "Are you sure you're not contagious?" I ask Mellie loudly. The girl scurries off and I turn back, lowering my voice. "We're only sixteen years old."

"There's no time like the present to DTR this situation," Mellie argues, not backing down. "If you know what you want, you should ask for it, Bailey. You're smart and funny and gorgeous, and any boy would be lucky to date you."

"You're my friend. You have to say that," I point out.

"True," Mellie says, looking down at her phone and texting. "But I also happen to mean it."

"I'm just really confused," I confess, letting my guard down now. Keeping my feelings bottled up about Jacob and Charlie is starting to wear on me. I decide to tell Mellie about my sledding date. To my shock, she barely blinks an eyelash.

"The way I see it, on the one hand, you've got an enigmatic Prince Charming with a British accent who seems to like you. On the other hand, you've got a guy you already know who is a bit of a dude but *did* take you to a Christmas tree farm and hold your hand, which means he likes you too.

"I mean, if it were me, I'd go with the guy with the accent. But then again, Jacob is pretty hot." Her eyes dart around. "Though I did hear a rumor we're supposed to be getting a group of exchange students from Finland in January. I wonder what kind of accent they'll have?"

"You aren't really helping me," I grumble.

"If you know what you want, you need to ask for it," Mellie says, making it all sound so simple. "Not knowing where you stand with a guy happens only if you allow it to happen and you'll be stuck in a situationship instead of a relationship. Okay, bye." She abruptly takes off down the hall before I can respond. "Radical honesty! It's a thing!" she shouts over her shoulder.

I text her the eye-roll emoji before I spin on my boot

heel and speed-walk over to my art class, just a few doors away from where we were huddled. For all the relationship advice Mellie dishes out, she has yet to have a serious boyfriend, unless you count this guy named George who she went out with the summer between freshman and sophomore years. They met on the boardwalk when she was on vacation with her mom at the Jersey Shore and had a long-distance relationship for two months before Mellie broke it off. So she's hardly an expert. And while I appreciate that a lot of this is filtered through her mom's situation, I don't think it really applies to me and Jacob.

We are less DTR and more MWD: Maybe We'll Date.

Besides, as much as I want to find a boy to kiss under the mistletoe, I don't like the idea of pushing a romance on him—or on anyone, for that matter. Because what if I do it and he walks away? Isn't it better to play it cool and leave the door open for a possible something rather than try to give it a label and risk him wanting nothing to do with me?

I take my usual seat at one of the middle wooden tables and smile at the other people who are already in the room. We are working on a drawing unit, using graphite and ink and colored pencils.

I share the Google Doc containing my character analysis chart for Hawthorne with Mellie, then find my art folder and take out the assignment I worked on last night. I smooth out the edges of the paper and add my name to the bottom corner. But while I am physically here in room 108, I am a million miles away in my mind. It's hard to stop thinking about Mellie and her well-meaning advice, as much as I didn't want to hear it.

In a daze, I gaze out the smudged classroom window. A bright red cardinal lands on a bare tree branch, sits still for a moment, then flies away, his little wings flapping hard. He is so free. On a whim, he can take off for places unknown. While here I sit, trapped in a high school classroom with a bunch of art students . . . and my thoughts.

"A lone woman is troubled with such dreams and such thoughts that she's afeared of herself sometimes."

The lone woman . . . is me.

Jacob. Charlie. Jacob. Charlie. What if every time I look at Jacob, I start thinking about Charlie and his amazing British accent? And when I'm with Charlie, what if Jacob and his picture-perfect Christmas tree farm won't get out of my head? DTR makes no sense. Because . . . how can I ask Jacob to define something that I can't define myself?

13

Wonderful Christmastime

"Tell me why I thought this was a good idea a week before Christmas," Victoria mutters as she stands surveying the scene with her hands on her hips. Tonight, Winslow's is hosting an author event. A fairly popular mystery writer will be here soon to give a short talk and sign copies of her latest book, *The Vermont Victim*. Carl and I had set up about forty folding chairs in the back area of the store for customers—we'd presold about thirty copies of *The Vermont Victim*, and are expecting a full house tonight. Winslow's has about seventy-five signings each year. Since I've worked here, we have had bestselling novelists, the former governor of Ohio, an athlete, some celebrities, and even a ten-year-old who wrote a book about American presidents. It's always exciting to have an author visit the store.

"Because it will increase foot traffic, a signed book is a great last-minute gift, and the last time Cressida White was here we sold out of her book?" Carl asks, making sure the mic at the podium is working. I put a glass of water next to it and a little cup of lozenges.

"Yes, fine, okay," Victoria says, frazzled. Bill is back preparing the "greenroom"—aka, the back room where we store boxes of books, eat meals between shifts, and leave our coats.

Fred the basset hound is curled up asleep in his bed up near the cash wrap area.

Tonight I'm supposed to be here as a gift wrapper, not a bookseller, but when I saw the frazzled look on Victoria's face, Sam had shooed me away from our table. Normally Victoria overschedules the staff for author events, but with everything going on for the holidays, she had spaced out and forgot. Only Carl, Irish Bill, and Tim, a bookseller with an insane knowledge of manga and sci-fi, are here. And now me. It has been a real mix-up.

Victoria checks her buzzing phone. "Oh, she's here!" She smooths down her black gingham tunic and dashes off to the front of the store.

I go over to the large rectangular table where we've stacked copies of *The Vermont Victim* and do some unnecessary straightening. We also had set up a table with bottles of water, glasses of wine, cubes of cheddar cheese with crackers, and green-iced cookies that are in the shape of Vermont, with tiny little splatters of fake blood on them.

"Do you like the cookies?" Tim asks, joining me. He walks with a slight limp—I don't know why and it isn't my business to ask.

"They're brilliant," I tell him, meaning it. "Your idea?"

He puffs out his skinny chest. "I wanted to do ice picks but didn't want to give away too much of the plot." He looks around to make sure no one is watching him, then picks up a cookie and gobbles it in three bites. "So are you a fan of Cressy White?" he asks, swallowing.

I pick up a copy of *The Vermont Victim*. The cover shows a woman obscured by shadows, opening a gated door. The title is embossed in gold script. "I haven't read any of her stuff," I admit, running my fingers over the title. "But this looks like a cool book."

Tim nods. "We sold a ton of her last one, *The Kansas Killer*. And considering that Vermont's a lot closer to us than Kansas is, and that she got a great review in the *Times*, this should do pretty well." He sighs. "I keep trying to convince Victoria to bring in more speculative fiction authors to do events. One day."

Customers who are here for the event begin filtering in, the brass shopkeeper's bell tinkling nonstop. There is excited chatter as people take their seats. A group of four women look especially enthusiastic. They all have glasses of wine. In the crowd I recognize one of the English teachers from Bedford High, and a couple who go to my church. You can almost feel the ripple of anticipation in the air as everyone waits for Cressida White to take the podium.

I hear Victoria's voice and the murmur of other voices. I carefully put the book back on the table and walk around the worn wooden bookshelves that block my view. A tall woman in a long white coat and stiletto boots is following Victoria through the shop, along with a younger woman in an oversized puffy jacket, white top, and black pants.

Victoria spots me lurking and motions me over. "Cressida, this is Bailey Briggs, one of your biggest fans."

I smile. "That's me!" I say cheerily. "I just can't get enough of murder mysteries." That's a bit of a fib, but I want to make Cressida feel good. We're all about author care at Winslow's.

Cressida and the younger woman, who I assume is her publicist, smile back at me. "Lovely to meet you," Cressida says, blinking her heavily mascaraed blue eyes. She smells like ripe bananas and coconut. "Love your top. And thanks for being a fan!"

The three of them head into the back. I hear Victoria ask if they're hungry and Cressida saying something about Whole30.

Back at the signing area, all the chairs are now filled.

Bill has pushed up some of the store's cushioned armchairs for extra seating. A few people stand on the sides but they seem content to stand.

"Did you read this one?" I ask him.

He rolls up his shirtsleeves and adjusts the pencil behind his ear. "Saw the ending coming a mile away." He holds up his finger to his lips. "Mum's the word, Bailey."

I laugh. "I'd hate to watch a true crime show with you."

Now Bill laughs. "I don't think you're the true crime type."

"I'm not." Sam has tried to get me to binge this show that Karl had told her about called *Homicide for the Holidays*—true crime cases that are holiday-themed.

Hard, hard pass.

When Cressida comes out, everyone applauds and she launches into a ten-minute reading of her book, followed by a Q&A. It was interesting, but six questions in, I wander up to the front of the store to check on Sam. It's pretty quiet at the wrap station—it seems that everyone in the store, even those people who haven't come specifically for the signing, are at the back listening to Cressida talk.

Sam points to the giant poster of Cressida's author photo we have on display at the front of the store. "Do you think anyone would notice if I give her a mustache?"

I giggle. "Victoria would probably have a heart attack right in front of us."

"I'm just a little bored up here. I'm glad this is our last night," she says, dropping into one of the folding chairs behind the table. I sit down at the other one. "I've been studying for APUSH but it's hard to concentrate with that." She motions toward where Cressida is speaking. Her miked voice carries throughout the store.

"It's fun to have an event on our last volunteer night, though," I point out. "Wonder how many people will want their books wrapped?"

"She's probably going to talk for another hour and

everyone is going to be so tired they'll just take their books and go home," Sam says. She makes a silly face and sends someone a Snapchat, then turns her phone camera on me. "Here, for Winslow's Instagram."

"If you hurry, you can still meet Cressida White tonight," I chirp, shimmying for the phone.

Sam turns the lens around toward her. "Come be a victim," she says in a dramatic voice, drawing a line across her throat. "A *Vermont Victim*."

"There's going to be a mad rush now," I say after we post the video to the store's Instagram account.

We spend some time scrolling Sam's Instagram account and watching videos. Then, when it sounds like Cressida might be finishing up, she puts her phone away.

"I almost forgot. You inspired me. I read a book." She held up a shelftalker she had written in purple Sharpie.

> Title: THE WILD
>   This book about a girl who gets sent to wilderness camp by her parents is, well, WILD.
> All sorts of things happen to her that she is NOT expecting—and neither will you!
>   I read this book in one day—you won't be able to put it down! —SAM

"I'm so proud of you! And that sounds so good," I tell her, even though thrillers give me nightmares. I haven't done any shelftalkers for a while, but I'm working on one for this book I borrowed from the store last week. It's kind of a choose-your-own-adventure romance—it is really funny. I considered doing one for a Dark Romantic from my English class just for kicks, but somehow trying to get someone to buy a dark story about someone trying and failing to make their lives better doesn't quite say "holiday spirit."

"So, I was at the mall over the weekend with my cousins and there was a seriously cute guy at the North Pole," Sam says. "Not that I'm interested." Ever since Joe Shiffley's party, she and Karl have been texting each other and sharing playlists. So far so good.

"Did he have a bushy white beard and a round belly?" I ask, resting my chin in my hands. "Do tell."

Sam ignores me. "Tall, blond hair that's long in the front—kind of like Leonardo DiCaprio before he got old and puffy. British accent."

I gasp, sitting back so hard in my chair I almost topple over backward. "Was his name Charlie?"

She's giving me a strange look as she shrugs. "I don't know. I didn't ask him. Why, do you know him or something?"

"I mean, I don't know if it's the same guy, but . . ." I trail off. "Wait—you didn't say what he was doing. Please tell me he wasn't Santa." The image that pops into my head is ludicrous.

"Nope. One of the elves." She chips off a piece of her blue nail polish. "My great-uncle used to work as a Santa during the holidays and he made decent money, something like twenty bucks an hour. He had to rent his own Santa suit, though."

Okay, Elf Charlie is even more ridiculous than him being Santa. "Like with tights and everything?"

Sam nods. "Full-on *A Christmas Story* Higbee's department store scene. Red tights, green top, floppy green hat with a jingle bell." She lets out a pained sigh. "If only I had a picture of him."

"Why don't you?" I screech, sounding a bit unhinged. All this time Charlie—my Charlie—worked at the mall as *an elf?* This would help explain why he isn't on social media—I am sure he doesn't want photos of himself in an elf outfit out in the world. When we were leaving Allen Park, he had been about to tell me something. This was probably it.

Sam gives me the universal "calm down" gesture with her hands. "I would have but my battery died."

Part of me doesn't want to believe it. The other part of me knows there aren't too many tall British guys who are good with kids in this town.

"Well, if it's the same person I'm thinking of, his name is Charlie Travers. We met at the ice rink a week ago, and then he helped me when my car got stuck on Big Tree Road," I tell her. "He just happened to be driving by at the right time."

"That's some coincidence," Sam says, sucking air through her teeth.

"Yeah," I say, thinking for a moment. "And last week he came in here."

"*Here* here?" Sam asks, her mouth forming a surprised O.

I nod. "We went sledding together with the kids I baby-sit for."

"That's so cute!" Sam cries, punching my arm. "But wait a minute. I thought you and Jacob Marley had a thing."

My shoulders slump. "I'm not sure if we do or not. He hasn't called what we have a thing, so—"

Sam cuts me off. "You should go to the North Pole and see if the elf is your Charlie."

My mom had offered to take me to the mall to shop for the Secret Santa gifts. I'd just have to make a small detour to visit the North Pole.

Tomorrow night can't come soon enough.

14

Santa Claus Is Comin' to Town

Most of the time my family shops locally in downtown Bedford. We like to support small businesses, and the center of town is just a short drive from our house. Tonight, however, we decide to go to the mall, mostly because it is too cold to be walking around outside. And when we pull into the parking lot of the Shoppes at Bedford, we realize everyone else has the same idea. The place is packed.

The Shoppes is a high-end shopping mall—there's valet parking and even a valet car wash. My mom refuses to use valet—"I'd have to be pretty desperate to pay fifteen dollars to park at *a mall* on a Tuesday!"—so we drove around for fifteen minutes before finally getting a parking spot.

Now we are walking down the expansive mall corridor. It's designed to look like a quaint outdoor street, complete with paved cobblestone floors and black iron streetlamps. Oversized jewel-toned ornaments are suspended from the ceiling, and the seating areas are festooned with cheery red poinsettias. There is an a cappella group singing outside a sporting goods store, and most of the display windows are lavishly decorated for the season. It's all very merry. On the news they are always talking about how malls are closing, but somehow, this one has managed to stay open. I notice a bunch of new stores since I was here last summer, and the food court has been remodeled to look like a chic urban space, with exposed pipes and reclaimed wood, which doesn't really go with the "Shoppes" vibe, but whatever— it's nice.

"What about lip gloss?" Mom says now as we approach Sephora. Inside the store, customers are spritzing on sweet-smelling perfumes and trying eye shadow colors on their arms. "Everyone likes lip gloss."

"Eh, I'm not sure. It feels . . . uninspired." Phoebe is one of my closest friends. I want to get her something really nice. As nice as a fifteen-dollar gift can be. Lip gloss feels generic, like a candle. It's the kind of gift you get someone when you can't think of anything else. And while I'm here to get a gift, I'm also here to see if I can learn a little more about the mysterious Charlie. So I'm a bit distracted. I glance around just in case he's in the vicinity, but I don't see him. If Sam was right, he is working at the North Pole. I can't really picture him as one of Santa's helpers, but I suppose anything is possible. Maybe they pay really well.

"Hmmmm, okay," Mom says, her neck swiveling from side to side as she studies the stores we are near. "Cute socks? A bracelet? Books? Think of what you'd like to get as a gift—and get Phoebe that."

She means well, but the more she suggests things, the more confused I grow. "No offense, Mom, but you're kind of stressing me out right now," I tell her as we wander into a giant cookware store, lured by the smell of hot mulled apple cider. "Just let me look around and I'll come up with something on my own."

Mom reaches over for a free sample of cider. "Just trying to help," she says, taking a sip from the small paper cup. "Delish. I wanted to look at the tablecloths here. Do you mind? I'll only be a minute."

I know Mom better than that—this place is dangerous for anyone her age. But I wave her off. "Sure, take your time," I say generously, glancing around at the shiny pots and pans and complicated-looking espresso machines. "Maybe I'll find something here for Phoebs."

"Okeydoke!" She meanders off, and I wander over to a festively decorated table covered in a green tablecloth. Each place setting has a charger, a dinner plate, a salad plate, a bread plate, a dessert plate, a soup bowl, three glasses, a teacup, nine utensils, and a reindeer napkin in a shiny silver ring. There is a gigantic pine cone centerpiece in the table's center.

"So bougie," I mumble, examining a gold-plated fork. Then I put it back and make my way over to a table with holiday treats. Maybe Phoebe would like a bag of gummies formed into snowmen. I pick up a bag that has a cute ribbon tied around it. The little sticker on the back says eighteen dollars. What a rip-off! I quickly put it back. This is just a waste of time. I glance toward the back of the store. Mom is having an animated conversation with an apron-wearing sales clerk, holding up a tartan place mat.

I pull out my phone from my back pocket and send my mom a text. I'll meet you by the fountain in fifteen minutes. Gonna walk around for a bit. 🌲 Then I squeeze my way past some shoppers and make my way back into the mall. If I can find something soon, then maybe I can do a quick surveillance trip to the North Pole.

I walk past an eyeglass shop, a men's shirt store, an Italian bistro, and a trendy athletic wear shop. I can see some cute patterned leggings and bright-colored sports bras inside, and there is a giant sign that says HOLIDAY SALE BUY ONE GET ONE 50% OFF. I hesitate. Phoebe does like to work out. Most of the merchandise is probably out of my price range, but maybe I can find a cute tank top on sale. I'm heading into the store when I hear it.

"Oh my God, stoooooop!" A girl's loud voice comes crashing down on my eardrums. My eyes follow the source of the piercing sound. I can't believe what I'm seeing. A few stores away from me is Jacob, along with Kaylee Zimmer and his ex, Jessica Dolecki. They're walking toward the athletic wear store, but they stop to check out a fancy-looking car on display in the center of mall. The girls are holding pink smoothies in clear plastic cups and laughing like they're in a comedy club and Jacob is the comedian.

An uncomfortable churning starts in my stomach. When I was in middle school, our social studies teacher assigned us to work in groups. I was unlucky enough to be put in a group with Kaylee and Jessica. We were supposed to come up with names for our groups. Jessica took one look at me and turned to Kaylee and said, "Let's call our group 'Two Pretty Girls and Bailey.'" Kaylee laughed super hard—exactly the way she's laughing now.

So I have valid reasons to pretty much despise them.

Jessica is twirling her long wavy hair around her finger, and Kaylee is holding on tight to Jacob's bicep. Jacob is laughing, too, but not quite as hard.

My eyes widen, and then narrow into tiny slits. Laughing is the furthest thing from my mind. Why on earth is Jacob at the mall with Kaylee and Jessica? Did he run into them? Or did they all come here together?

I move back out into the mall corridor to get a better view.

Jacob must have said something, because Kaylee laughs her annoying loud laugh again, miming spitting out her smoothie. "Stop, stop, oh my gosh," she shrieks, flipping her blowout from side to side. Her head turns in my direction and I duck behind a life-sized nutcracker statue. I can only imagine what will happen if they see me. Either the girls would blow me off like they don't know who I am (never mind that we've been in classes together since second grade) or they'd make a big show of saying hi and then whispering to each other and laughing afterward to try to make me feel insecure. And this would all play out in front of Jacob—and as for what he would do, I don't really want to find out.

I peek out from behind the nutcracker. I don't see Kaylee and Jessica, which is both a relief and a bit disappointing, because Jacob has vanished as well. Knowing them, the girls have probably gone into Starbucks to order single venti iced mochas, no whip, light ice, and 2 percent milk before yelling at the baristas that they made their drinks wrong.

But where is Jacob? He had mentioned something about needing a new band for his Apple watch. Is he in the Apple store? Even from this far away, I can tell it's crowded.

A text from my mom pops up. Sorry I'm taking so long. They're trying to find a 90-inch round tablecloth for me down in their stockroom. Do you want to still meet at the fountain? Say 30 minutes?

Sounds good! I type back. As much as I don't like seeing Jacob hanging out with those mean girls, I know I shouldn't devote any time to worrying about it. Whether he came here alone and ran into them or planned to meet up with them isn't really my business anyway. I let out a breath I hadn't realized I was holding.

I have to focus. I need to get Phoebe's gift. And I need to see if Charlie is in an elf costume.

15

Let It Snow

After finding the perfect gift at a kiosk—a set of firefly string lights that I know Phoebe will love—I head for the North Pole. You'd think there wouldn't be a line because it's a weeknight, but it is also just a few days before Christmas, which means a decent-sized crowd is waiting to go in. There's an open area with benches and large candy cane decorations, and a path cordoned off by red velvet ropes that lead past a small kiosk. Past the kiosk is the North Pole and, I'm assuming, Santa.

I stand in line behind two moms with little kids. Slowly the line inches forward.

"Hi! Welcome to the North Pole," a college-aged girl says to me when I reach the check-in booth. "Were you interested in a photo package? Our cheapest is the twenty-six-dollar Little Elf package. There's the thirty-five-dollar Jolly Snowman, and then the fifty-dollar Reindeer Blitz, which includes—"

"Nope, no photos," I interrupt, and she instantly stops talking. "Um, I just wondered—does a guy named Charlie work here?"

The girl shrugs. "Maybe? I never can remember anyone's names. You can go into the North Pole and look around if you want to."

I smile at her. "Okay, thanks." I walk ahead to the Toy Workshop—a temporary "room" with large-screen TVs playing animated videos of elves carving wood into toys, complete with a jaunty soundtrack. In the middle is a large table with several different wooden toys and games that kids are playing with. I'm a little surprised the kids aren't more eager to go see Santa, but I guess a lot of kids are afraid of him.

I pass through the snow room and into the Winter Wonderland section, which consists of piles of fake snow, kids tossing snow at each other, and kids making snow angels, all while the classic version of "Winter Wonderland" by Johnny Mathis plays overhead.

And there, past Winter Wonderland, is Santa. He's seated atop a large, ornate throne, and there is a line of children waiting to sit on his lap. I don't know where the Shoppes at Bedford found him, but this Santa is perfect. He has a fluffy white beard, a pair of wire-rimmed glasses that slide down his nose, and a very round belly that looks like the product of too many of Mrs. Claus's homemade goodies instead of fake padding. He's wearing a plush red Santa suit, white gloves, and a pair of shiny black boots.

A little girl in a fancy party dress is sitting on Santa's lap, screaming her head off. The North Pole photographer is snapping away.

"It's Santa! Remember, Ava? We've been talking about visiting him all week!" Ava's mom hovers a few feet away, looking exasperated. But Ava isn't having it.

"I'm so sorry," the mom apologizes to Santa. "I really thought she was ready."

Santa chuckles. "Ho, ho, ho, no need to apologize. Ava might just not feel like talking to me today. But I do have something to give her, to thank her for coming to see me today." He looks over to the side and out of the wings comes a male elf. Tall, blond, adorable.

Charlie.

He walks straight over to Ava and crouches down to her level, offering her a candy cane. "Hi, Ava. I'm Charlie. Santa's helper."

The little girl stares up at him. *I know the feeling, Ava*, I think. Except I've never seen Charlie quite like this.

He's wearing a green velvet jacket with peppermint buttons, cinched with a black belt. The jacket has white fur trim at the collar and cuffs. Bright red pants with green rickrack stripes balloon out and taper below his knees, and he has on red-and-green-striped socks that tuck into the most ridiculously curled toe boots.

It's a lot to drink in.

Ava stops crying and reaches for the treat. "Thank you," she whispers, hiccupping.

Santa smiles down at her. "I heard you've been doing very well in ballet this year," Santa says. "Do you want to tell us about it?"

And just like that, the tears stop and the little girl's face lights up in wonder. I watch, astonished, as she and Santa chat, while Charlie listens attentively on the side. I'm unable to hear what she is saying, but Charlie is smiling, and Santa even does a big belly laugh, his hands on his stomach.

I look around at everyone in line and we're all smiling at one another, our spirits lifted. It's Christmas Magic.

"Wow. Thank you, Santa!" the mom exclaims when Ava hops off his lap and scampers over to her. "That was . . . that was amazing!"

"Ho, ho, ho! Merry Christmas!" Santa replies, giving them a kindly wave before squirting some hand sanitizer on his palms. Ava waves back before reaching for her mom's hand. They head for the exit.

"Now, who do we have here?" Santa asks, peering over the rim of his glasses and looking in my direction. "Would you like to come sit on Santa's lap?"

Is he talking to me? I turn around, and the family behind me smiles encouragingly and motions for me to go up. "Oh, um, I wasn't expecting this," I say, suddenly feeling shy.

Charlie has noticed me by now. "You're never too old for Santa," he calls out, and the family behind me eggs me on.

"Well, okay," I say sheepishly. I walk up to Santa and perch tentatively on his knee.

Santa puts his hands on his hips. "Ho, ho, ho, it's wonderful to see you, Bailey. How have you been?"

"Oh, gee. Well, I've been good," I hear myself say. I look over at Charlie, who is standing a few feet behind Santa. He wears a bemused, slightly unreadable expression. I'm not sure how Charlie told Santa my name without my seeing him do it. Impressive.

Santa bends his head toward mine. His breath is warm and minty. "So, what are you hoping to get in your stocking on Christmas morning?"

The last time I visited Santa was in third grade. Being back on Santa's lap is giving me all the feelings. "Well, it's not so much something in my stocking. I . . . I'm hoping for some Christmas Magic," I confess under my breath. "You know, like—"

Santa's face lights up and he holds up a hand to cut me off. "Say no more, dear. You don't want another bottle of perfume or a gift card. No, you want something deeper. Meaningful."

I nod. "Yes. Exactly."

"You're searching for the wonder of Christmas in a child's eyes," Santa continues, a yearning in his tone. "The traditions that fill home with laughter and make forever memories."

"*Yes*," I say emphatically. This Santa really gets me.

"Have you watched any Christmas movies? Baked cookies? Drunk hot cocoa?"

"*Miracle on 34th Street, Elf, Home Alone*," I rattle off. "And yes, cookies and hot cocoa on the regular."

"Good, good." Santa thoughtfully taps his white-bearded chin. "Have you driven around town to see the lights?"

"Not yet," I tell him. "But I will!"

"Go! It will make your spirits bright," Santa urges. "And don't forget to leave food for the reindeer in your yard on Christmas Eve."

"Rudolph can count on me, Santa," I promise. Who can say no to Santa Claus?

Santa smiles, and it reaches the corners of his eyes. "I can see that you are filled with the Christmas spirit, Bailey. Never stop believing in the magic of Christmas." He stares deep into my Christmas-loving soul. "Something tells me you just might get your wish and more this year."

I'm overwhelmed with feelings of goodwill and good cheer. It's a good thing Charlie materializes next to Santa or I might have stayed here forever. "Bailey, unfortunately your time with Santa is up," he says. "Time for your next guest, sir," he tells Santa.

I take the cellophane-wrapped candy cane Charlie hands me. "Thank you, Santa," I say, beaming at him.

"Merry Christmas, Bailey," he replies, giving me a wink.

Charlie gives me his hand and helps me to my feet. It's a good thing too—I feel dazed and dizzy after my time with Santa, like I've walked into the shade after standing in blinding sunlight. "Here, I'll walk you out," he says as twin boys race past us and dive onto Santa's lap. I can hear Santa chuckling as we leave.

"He's a perfect Santa," I say, letting out a contented sigh.

"He is, isn't he?" Charlie agrees. "Quite the jolly old fellow. He told me this is his tenth year at the mall."

"Well, he's a keeper," I say.

"I was surprised to see you here tonight," Charlie says. "Most of our North Pole guests are, well—"

"Younger?" I finish for him. "You can say it. I'm not offended. I wear my love of all things Christmas proudly. It's a badge of honor."

He nods. "As someone who is wearing a green elf jacket and pointy-toed elf boots, I completely respect that."

"And speaking of surprises—you never told me you work here!" I exclaim.

"Well, I didn't want to mention it in front of the kids the other day and ruin their innocence," Charlie tells me.

I hadn't thought of that. "Ahhh. That makes sense," I say. "You said you wanted to tell me something when we were leaving Allen Park and I thought maybe this was it."

He shrugs. "Funny, I don't remember what it was now. So tell me what brought you to the North Pole tonight."

"Well I didn't come here expecting to sit on Santa's lap," I say truthfully.

He raises an eyebrow. "Were you expecting someone else? Say . . . the Easter Bunny?"

I know he's teasing me—but obviously there is no way I can tell him the truth: that I came here to see if he was an elf. "I'm, um, writing an article for my school newspaper about the commercialization of Christmas. How . . . how the season becomes more about getting new cool stuff instead of what's important. I was just checking out the scene over here when Santa waved me over."

"That sounds interesting," Charlie says. "But you know what? I don't believe people *have* lost the meaning of Christmas."

I look up at him. "You don't?"

He shakes his head. "Sure, there are kids who ask Santa for expensive video games and phones. But there are also a lot of kids who ask for things like winter boots. Or for their soldier dad to come home from overseas. Or for money so their mom doesn't have to work two jobs just to put food on the dinner table."

"Wow," I say softly. "That's rough." But I can understand it. Santa is the one person you feel safe talking to and confiding in. And if my experience is any indication, the Santa here at the mall is exactly who kids need to confide in.

"So what did you ask the big guy for?" Charlie asks, interrupting my thoughts. He looks down at me as we walk toward the exit.

"As Santa's helper, you should know better than to ask me that," I kid. I'm going to keep that Christmas Magic conversation to myself. "But I do have a question to ask you: how are you walking in those shoes?"

Charlie gives a stomp and the small bells on the top of the shoe jangle. "Practice makes perfect, I suppose."

"How long have you worked here?" I ask. It isn't fair—even in a dorky elf outfit, Charlie looks good.

"Not long . . . just a couple weeks. They were short on elves this year and it's crunch time."

I try to imagine Jacob in the elf costume. The mental picture is just too much. I can't help it—I laugh.

Charlie raises his eyebrows. "Ignore me," I tell him, brushing away the thought. "Just thinking of, um, something funny my mom said to me."

"I thought maybe you were laughing at my costume," he says, giving me a sidelong glance.

"What? No! I mean, people would kill to get to wear a getup like that," I say, which might have been a bit of a stretch. "How did you even get the job?"

He gives one of his peppermint buttons a tug. "I'm very conscientious and have a great eye for detail. I told Santa I could help him check all his lists twice." He drops his voice. "And . . . it probably helped that I fit into the elf uniform and am strong enough to help lift all the kids who want to sit on Santa's lap but can't quite reach him." He flexes his arm. "You'd be surprised at what a workout it is."

I imagine Charlie using toddlers like five-pound weights, lifting them over his head, and giggled. "I hear that the North Pole workout is all the rage," I say, going along with it. "So tell me, was I on the nice or naughty list?"

"Definitely the nice list, Bailey Briggs," Charlie says, his expression suddenly serious. "No coal is ever going in your stocking on Christmas morning."

His intensity takes me a little by surprise. "Oh," I say. "Well, that's good. Better than being on the naughty list!" Ooof. Could I sound any more awkward? Thankfully we have reached the North Pole exit.

"Very true." He glances back at Santa. "I'd better get back to work. Once Santa finishes up, it's my job to get him out of the mall and on his way before he gets stopped by any of his fans."

To be honest, I want to stop Santa myself. He was so easy to talk to, and seemed so wise. And it feels good to meet up with Charlie, who loves Christmas as much as I do. "You're kind of like Santa's bouncer," I tell him.

Charlie nods. "I mean, he is a bit of a rock star at this time of year—but he also needs his sleep." Charlie's dimple twitches, giving me butterflies. "He's got a big night ahead of him. He needs his rest."

My phone dings. Did you get lost? Followed by another text, this one my mom's Bitmoji peering from behind a hedge of leaves.

Mom. I completely forgot about her. Sorry! Coming! I text back.

"Would you want to hang out after school tomorrow?" Charlie asks me. "There's something I want to show you that I think you'll like."

Tomorrow is the last day of school before winter break. "Sounds fun," I say to him. "Can you at least give me a hint?"

But he shakes his head. "You'll just have to wait and see."

16

God Rest Ye Merry Gentlemen

The last day of school before our two-week break goes by in its usual blur, with a rush of before-the-break quizzes, final assignments, and a plea by our homeroom teacher not to leave anything in our lockers that could be covered with mold when we come back in January. Eddie Lascola left what appeared to have been a peach and a sesame bagel with cream cheese last year and the entire wing had to be disinfected when school reopened.

I kept my eyes peeled for Jacob today, but I didn't see him once. I want to know if he went to the mall last night with Jessica and Kaylee, but I'm not about to text him to ask. Not that I should care, really. It isn't like we are officially dating or anything. I mean, here I am now, with Charlie, on our date. Or whatever it is.

"So, how did you get involved with this place?" I ask Charlie. We're standing in front of a large artificial Christmas tree in the community room of the Stewart Senior Center.

Charlie had texted me the address and Caitlin had dropped me off on her way to her SAT prep class. When Charlie asked if we could meet up here, I thought it was some kind of hangout place for high school seniors. But no, the center is for actual *senior citizens*—as in, people over the age of seventy. I felt a little weird walking in alone, but the minute I saw Charlie standing next to the lobby reception desk, a happy peaceful feeling came over me. He gave me a hug, introduced me to Jeanette, the receptionist, and led me down the hall to "the gathering room."

Underneath my parka, I have on a pair of joggers, a button-up top, Kar's denim jacket, and an infinity scarf. I feel pretty cute. And Charlie *looks* pretty cute. He has on a navy sweater with the sleeves pushed up, jeans, and leather loafers that have just the right amount of scuff. By the appreciative looks and smiles of the elderly residents, he has totally charmed them as well. He always looks comfortable and at ease—even in an elf costume. I think that says a lot about a person.

The tree in front of us is trimmed, but not with holiday decorations. Instead, there are around a dozen or so ornament tags made from colored paper hanging on the tree, cut in the shape of trees, angels, and wreaths. Each one is numbered and has an individual's first name, their age, and the gift they are hoping to receive for Christmas.

"I have a friend here who told me about it," Charlie says. "Each year they receive hundreds of requests from local organizations who are hoping to brighten someone's holiday."

"A friend?" I look around us, searching for who Charlie could be referring to. A lady with short white hair is sitting on a couch doing a crossword puzzle. An older gentleman in a plaid shirt, gray pants held up with a belt, and slippers is slowly pushing a walker across the room toward a large-screen TV that is turned to a news station. A few women are drinking coffee and playing some sort of card game together.

Charlie nods. "Friends come in all shapes and sizes, you know."

"Oh, of course!" I exclaim, feeling called out. "I just . . . I guess I don't have too many friends who aren't my age."

The man with the walker spots Charlie. "Nice to see you, Charlie!"

Charlie waves back. "Hey, Mr. Radcliffe. Glad to see you up and moving. Keep it up!"

Mr. Radcliffe pretends to tip his hat. "I'll do my best!"

"So that's your friend?" I ask, smiling.

Charlie smiles back. "One of them." He turns his attention to the tree and takes an angel tag off. "Jade. Age fourteen. She wants a blue sweatshirt and a pair of sneakers."

I have also taken a tag off—a wreath. "This one is for Reya. She's sixty. She wants . . ." I pause. "She wants fabric softener and laundry detergent pods." I feel a lump form in my throat at the idea of a sixty-year-old woman asking for those things as her Christmas present.

"This makes me so sad," I whisper, clutching the tag. "Laundry pods for Christmas?" I think of the things my family typically exchanges with each other as we sit in front of our fireplace in our Christmas jammies—sweaters and perfume and electronics, frivolous things like foot massagers and gold bracelets that we don't really need. Books and games and gift cards. Not household items like detergent. "It's just not right."

Charlie sighs, pushing his sweater sleeves up. "I know. There are so many people out there who have so little. It's easy not to see them when we get caught up in our busy lives."

I look around, wondering if Reya is one of the ladies playing cards. "Do all the tags come from people who live here?"

Charlie shakes his head. "No. Some of them are Stewart residents, but each year they help out different organizations. Usually it's a mix of residential homes for people with physical disabilities and schools and retirement homes." He holds up his tag. "Schools get angel tags, the residential homes get the wreaths, and the residents of the retirement homes get the trees."

I didn't think it was possible, but being here puts me even more in the holiday mood. I love all the traditions I have with my friends and family, but it feels good to think outside of myself and help someone who might not have such a good Christmas.

"I think this is the one I'm going to take." Charlie lifts a tag off a tree. *Richard, 83, a power cord and AAA batteries.* "And I might just have to supplement it with an electric blanket . . . and maybe a winter coat," he says, a twinkle in his eye.

My eyes widen. I didn't realize you can buy things other than what's on the tag. But why not? The holidays are all about generosity and kindness. And really, how can you just give someone a power cord? Nothing says "bah humbug" like an eight-pack of batteries.

The lady who had been working on the crossword puzzle comes over to us. "It's so nice to see young people doing good deeds," she says, touching my arm. She smells like lavender. "Makes my heart happy. Also, I love your scarf!"

I smile at her. Old people are so cute. They make me think of my grandpa. "It makes my heart happy too. And thank you."

"Margie, hello!" the lady says, greeting a woman who works there as she walks by, a cheerful smile on her face.

"Thanks for your help organizing the gift table, Louise," Margie says, nodding across the room. "Can't wait until we get to pass them all out."

Louise winks. "Well, we don't get to do it. Santa does, remember."

Margie winks back. "Ahhh, that's right—the man with the bag!" She hurries off down the corridor.

Louise points over to a folding table that contains a small pile of wrapped gifts. "All you need to do is enter the number of your tag into this book and bring the wrapped gift back by Friday at seven p.m. with the tag taped to it. No bows."

"Friday?" I repeat. That makes sense—obviously they have to get the gifts back before Christmas so there is enough time to pass them out—but that's just two days away. There are a lot of tags still on the tree.

"So what happens to the tags that aren't taken off the tree?" I ask, furrowing my brow. I'm afraid to find out the answer.

Louise lets out a long sigh. "Well, it's what you'd expect—they won't get gifts." I can tell it bothers her—and it bothers me too. I reach up and take one tag off. And then another. And another. Jade and Reya and Richard and Chiara and Javante and Sydney . . . I'm not sure how I am going to pay for all of them, but the holiday spirit has come over me and I just can't stop. I am a tag-taking machine.

Louise has been watching me and now she lets out a little gasp. "Oh my goodness. Girls!" She gestures to the other residents. "Look what they're doing." She lowers her voice. "Don't let him get away," she tells me, pointing at Charlie, who thankfully is talking with Mr. Radcliffe. "A young man as kindhearted as he is? He's almost too good to be true!" She pinches my cheek. "And you—you're an absolute doll. Charlie, she's a beauty and generous—this one's a keeper!"

Charlie looks over at us and laughs. "I wouldn't argue with that, Louise." He reaches out and takes the few remaining tags off the tree. "Like I said the other day," he says, looking at me with his warm hazel eyes that could reach into the depths of my soul and send a kaleidoscope of butterflies loose in my chest, "Bailey Briggs, you are forever and always on the nice list."

· · ·

When I get home from the Stewart Center, I'm just in time for dinner ... kind of. My family has all waited for me and everyone is a little salty about it.

"I never said you had to wait," I say, piling some baked rigatoni on my plate. "Don't make me the bad guy."

Liam just grabs a crescent roll and grunts—he is too busy eating to argue with me. Karolyn rolls her eyes as she pours ranch dressing on her salad. "While you were out with your friends, you missed all the fun. Unloading the dishwasher, setting the table, chopping celery ..."

Thankfully my parents are too busy chattering about problems at their jobs, the stock market, and dentist appointments—they aren't paying any attention to what my sister is saying. So much for quality time at family dinners.

"I wasn't with my friends," I whisper under my breath. "If you have to know ... I was out with this guy." I shoot a look at Liam to make sure he isn't listening. When it comes to my dating life, he is strictly on a need-to-know basis. And he rarely, if ever, needs to know. "And we were doing a good deed."

"Like what?" Kar asks, arching an eyebrow.

"Cheering up senior citizens." I give her the two-minute version of my time at the Stewart Center.

But to my surprise, my sister doesn't look impressed. "Santa's nice list isn't actually a thing, Bailey. You aren't going to get service points for helping a bunch of old people."

Now Dad is stressing to Mom the importance of getting an oil change before the end of the year. I gape at my sister. "I can't believe you just said that."

"Yeah, well, most people stop believing in Santa when they're—"

I wave my fork at her, sending a rigatoni noodle flying onto my place mat. "Not that, but that's a whole other level of nonsense." I blow out a hot, angry breath at my sister's insensitive words. "I wasn't doing this for 'service points,'" I insist. "I was doing it because the person I was meeting thought it might be a fun way to spend the afternoon while at the same time doing something good for someone else."

Karolyn holds up her hands. "Okay, okay. Sorry. I wasn't trying to make you all mad or anything. Chill."

"You chill," I tell her, shaking my head.

She takes a dainty bite of salad. "So who's the person you were meeting, anyway?" she asks at the same time Mom asks, "Who wants more pasta?" and holds up a silver serving spoon.

I wipe my lips on my napkin. "Not me—I'm full. Thanks, Mom." I leave the table to go rinse off my dishes in the sink. Dickens trots over, hoping for a crumb. I pat his soft white head instead.

"You didn't answer my question," Karolyn says, coming up behind me. "Who were you with?"

"This guy I met a couple weeks ago," I tell her, opening the dishwasher and putting my silverware inside.

My sister whips out her phone, her finger hovering over the buttons. "Is he in your grade? What's his name?"

I shake my head. "He doesn't go to Bedford and he's not on social media."

Karolyn's eyes widen, as if I've just told her Charlie is a bank robber. "That's so weird."

I shrug. "I think it's kind of cool," I tell her. I don't think it's weird, exactly, but I would have liked to stalk him a little if I could. "Guess he just likes his privacy."

She mulls this over. "It does make him kind of mysterious."

"It does, doesn't it," I say thoughtfully. But after my sister leaves the room, I take out my phone. Louise had taken a photo of the two of us today, standing in front of the tree, holding our tags and smiling for the camera. She only took one picture, but thankfully it was in focus. There's something about Charlie's eyes that pull me in . . . but keep me at arm's length.

I can't shake the feeling that Charlie has a lot more secrets—just like that hidden lion tattoo—up his sweatered sleeve.

17

Have Yourself a Merry Little Christmas

The next morning, I wake up with a start and throw off my comfy down comforter before realizing this isn't a normal school day and I don't have to get up at the crack of dawn. Sighing, I flop back on my flannel sheets, pulling my pillow toward me in a happy hug. "No more school for two weeks," I whisper, yawning before falling back asleep for three more hours.

When I finally reopen my eyes, the sun is streaming through my half-raised shades. The house is completely silent. I pick up my phone and look at our family group chat. My parents are at work, Liam is out for a run, and Karolyn is out to breakfast with her friends. Having the house all to myself is a rare and special occasion. I slide out of bed and pad down to the kitchen in my T-shirt and shorts. Dickens is asleep in his beanbag and barely lifts his head when I walk in.

I pour myself a glass of orange juice and pop a slice of

rye bread into the toaster. Today I have to shop until I drop. The Stewart Center gifts need to be turned in tomorrow—Louise reminded me of this several times when I signed the book. The pile of gift tags is where I left it, on the desk in our kitchen.

I pick it up and look at each tag. Some of the items aren't too expensive—the batteries, mascara, a pair of gloves. But some things do sound a little out of my price range. I chew on my cuticle. I don't have a great sense of how much things cost. Like . . . how much is a queen-sized comforter? Or a Packers jersey? Or a soccer ball and cleats?

Trying not to panic, I turn on the TV on our kitchen counter. "The countdown is on," the perky reporter is saying. She is standing in the middle of a crowded shopping mall. "If you didn't take advantage of all that free holiday delivery we told you about last week, guys, well, you've most likely missed the window with most retailers. Unless you're willing to pay big bucks for expedited delivery—and no guarantees that packages will reach you on time—you're going to have to do your shopping the old-fashioned way. Fighting through the hustle and bustle. Jim, back to you in the studio!"

"What was I thinking?" I mumble, cradling my head in my hands. Yesterday I'd been swept up in Christmas Magic. Today I am facing Christmas Fear. It had taken me forever to pick out the string of fairy lights to give to Phoebe. The good thing is I don't have to guess what people want—it's all spelled out on the tags—but how long is it going to take to find all these things? It's probably too late to order on-line, and there's definitely no room in my budget for rush shipping fees.

My phone buzzes. It's a Snap from Jacob. His face looms large on my screen. So there's this thing called Holiday Carnival reads the caption in the Glow font.

Wow. After a few days without seeing him, I wasn't expecting to wake up to this. I immediately send him an equivalent Snap of my face with a caption that reads I'm familiar with it and add an avocado sticker over my mouth.

Another picture of his face, this time with the psyche-delic glasses filter. Do you want to go with me?

I hesitate, the conversation I'd had with Mellie the other day ringing in my ears. It has been a few days since I've seen Jacob. Does that mean he doesn't *like me*, like me? Or does it mean he was just busy? Maybe he just wants to be friends and is asking me as a friend. Not everything has to mean something.

I think back to our day together at Marleys' Christmas Tree Farm. The trees, the snow, the tree tag—it was awe-some. But then I think back to the day I went sledding with Charlie and the Parker kids. That had been a really fun day too.

Technically there is no reason why I can't go to the car-nival with Jacob. I've heard people talking about it at school and it sounds really fun. But part of me feels guilty, as if I'm somehow cheating on Charlie if I spend time with Jacob. Would Charlie's feelings be hurt if he knew I was spending the day with Jacob? Or would Jacob get offended if he knew I spent yesterday with Charlie? Relationships are so confusing.

You could just DTR it, the Mellie in my mind reminded me.

"No," I whisper angrily to Mind Mellie. I am not about to ask Jacob to DTR our relationship. Or our situationship. Our whatevership.

Something had occurred to me last night. I was texting my friends and finally telling them a little more about my friendship with Charlie—I'd decided it wasn't right to only confide in Mellie—and how we'd gone to the Stewart Center together. The truth—and it is a little disconcerting to admit it—is that nothing remotely romantic has happened between me and Charlie. No holding hands, no kissing, not even any *Oops, we were almost kissing* moments. Sure, the *situations* we have been in are romantic, and Charlie and his dimples are about the hottest things I've ever seen, but when I think about it, all our interactions have been totally platonic. Our last "date" together was at a retirement home, for Pete's sake.

Am I reading into something that isn't even there?

Rut-ro.

A Snapchat message pops up. Yo you still there?

And even though I should be freaking out about all the gifts I have to buy, a strange calmness settles over me. Don't ask me how, but I instinctively know everything is going to work out okay. After all, good things always happen at

Christmas—and Santa told me never to stop believing in the magic.

I chug the rest of my juice and put the glass down so hard on the counter, Dickens's head pops up like a prairie dog's. What time can you pick me up?

. . .

The Holiday Carnival is in full swing by the time we arrive and park the truck in a makeshift parking lot in a field. There are aisles of jewelry, pottery, candles, quirky art prints, and holiday crafts from a variety of vendors, all set up in cozy temporary stalls. Garlands frame the stall entrances, and overhead, strings of large holiday bulbs zigzag, giving the market a festive glow. The familiar notes of *A Charlie Brown Christmas* play over tinny-sounding speakers.

"Wait, where is that hot chocolate place?" Jacob asks as we pass a stall selling leather belts and cross-body bags. He hasn't held my hand today, but he purposefully knocked into my shoulder a couple times, pulled my ponytail, and rested his chin on my shoulder while we were waiting in one of the food lines. It *seems* like he's trying to be close to me. I'm deliberating asking him about the other day at the mall. I'm dying to know if he went there with Kaylee and Jessica. But I don't want to bring it up and ruin the fun we're having.

I blink in amazement as I watch him look in earnest for the hot chocolate stall. "Seriously? I'm so stuffed!" We already shared a paper boat filled with maple glazed mini-doughnuts, truffle fries, and a warm pull-apart pretzel, washing it all down with hot mulled cider.

He rubs his stomach. "Bottomless pit and proud of it."

I groan as we pass a cart selling caramel-covered apples. "I don't even want to see food."

"So . . . I guess that means stopping at the diner later is out of the question?" Jacob tries putting his hands together like he's praying.

I dead-eye him. "Not answering that."

We've been here long enough that the sun is slowly setting. I am starting to get a little cold in my chunky sweater and skinny jeans, and my boots are pinching my toes. The lights above the stalls have turned on, making everything look extra fairylike now.

I take out my phone to check the time. It's 5:30. As much as I'm having a good time, I have to get home. I decide I'm going to come clean to my parents and tell them about the gift tags. They won't be happy, but they can't argue with my good intentions. We'll have to hit one of the superstores that's open for late-night shopping. But I'm not about to let Louise or the other residents down.

At the end of the aisle, we come to an outdoor ice-skating rink framed by a white picket fence. Couples are holding hands and smiling as they skate past us. Jacob rolls his eyes. "So cliché, right? Holiday skating rink."

I shrug. "I think it's nice."

"Oh," Jacob says, sounding surprised. "Are you a good skater?"

"Mmmm, I wouldn't go that far," I say, remembering the last time I was on the ice—the day I met Charlie. "But I think it's a fun thing to do."

"So are you saying you want to skate?" Jacob asks me.

I shake my head. I could literally feel the junk food sloshing around in my stomach. "I just like watching. I make up stories in my head about the people."

Jacob grins. "Love that. Okay, what's their deal?" He points to a guy and girl who look like they are in college. They are very good skaters. The girl has on a skate skirt and tights.

I tap my chin. "Okay, he's very into skating and secretly wishes he could go to the Olympics. She feels the same way about the Olympics, but she's not interested in him romantically. But neither of them has told the other how they feel."

Jacob nods. "I could believe that. What about them?" This time he is looking at a couple who are probably my parents' age. The man is tall with a goatee, and the woman has short blond hair and is wearing a bright magenta jacket. They are skating really slowly and the woman is laughing a lot.

"First date," I say confidently. "She wanted to do something fun in case she ran out of things to say to him. He's just happy to be out on a date—he hasn't dated much since his wife left him for their plumber."

"And how's it going?" Jacob asks, leaning against the fence. "Their date, I mean."

"Very well," I say as the man reaches for the blond woman's hand. "In fact, I wouldn't be surprised if he tries to kiss her right out there on the ice. It's the quintessential spot for a first-date kiss."

Jacob isn't looking at the ice rink anymore. Instead, he is staring right at me. "Wait," he says, cupping my face with his hand.

My breath kind of hiccups in my throat. What is happening right now? Never breaking our gaze, he reaches up and brushes my cheek with his fingertips. "You have some serious doughnut crumbs on your face."

I wrinkle my nose, self-conscious. "I do?"

"Mmm-hmm. A *lot* of them. They're gone now."

I instinctively reach up and touch my own cheek. "Uh, okay."

"You sound like you don't believe me," he says. "Why would I make it up?"

I shrug. "I didn't say that you did."

"I mean, it's not like I needed an excuse to reach over and touch your cheek, you know."

"Uh, okay," I say again. Suddenly my vocabulary has shrunk to a handful of words.

We've had a lot of fun together today. Jacob likes to joke around a lot and he is pretty funny. Spending time with him is easy to do. But now I suddenly feel shy. Maybe it's because we're talking about first dates and kissing and doughnut crumbs.

"If someone is watching the two of us, what do you think they'd say?" Jacob asks, crossing his arms.

"Hmmmm," I say, taking the question seriously. I've never put myself into the "voyeuree" role. "Um, I think they'd think we were friends from school, by the way we're laughing and looking comfortable together."

"True that," Jacob says, prodding me along. "Go on."

"And they'd guess that I'm the more serious one, while you're a bit of a jokester."

Jacob gives me a grin. "Speak the truth, you do. So you think we're that easy to read, huh?"

"Yes," I say with a sigh. "I wish I could say we were more mysterious, but . . . it is what it is."

"Interesting," he replies, moving closer to me. "But what I really want to know," he says softly, "is if we're so easy to read, did anyone see this coming?" And before I know what's happening, his maple-glazed, truffle-coated, salty lips are on mine.

And I never saw it coming.

18

Jingle Bells

Kissing Jacob Marley isn't anything like I expected it to be.

It's better. His full lips are soft, and his breath is a mixture of maple and cinnamon. I reach up and put my hands on his chest and he wraps his arms around my lower back.

I haven't kissed anyone since Oliver and I broke up, and now I wonder if what Oliver and I did could even be called kissing. Making out with Oliver was more like a mashing-up of lips and Oliver opening his mouth way too wide and once actually covering my nose, which is as disgusting as it sounds.

Jacob kisses like he really cares about kissing and wants to do a good job of it. And he is.

When we pull apart, I don't know what to do or what to say. My lips are tingling, and my hands feel all fluttery, so I stuff them in my jacket pocket.

Jacob clears his throat. "Was that okay?"

I give a rapid nod. "Totally okay."

He breaks into a grin. "Okay. Good. I've been wanting to do that for a long time."

"You have?" I say, swallowing. I can't believe we just kissed!

"You're a great kisser," Jacob tells me.

I can feel my cheeks warm up. "You are too," I blurt out. I feel kind of self-conscious but Jacob seems totally at ease. He looks down at the ground and then his eyes shoot up to meet mine. "I mean, you know I like you, Bailey. I think it's been pretty obvious."

At this point I know the right thing to do would be to nod or smile, to maybe even lean back in and kiss him. And I feel like doing all of those things at this very moment. But I can't stop reliving the moment in the mall from the other night, when he was with two of the meanest girls at my school, one of them his former girlfriend. And that's when I do the absolute worst thing I could do.

"So I've been wondering . . . what were you doing with Kaylee and Jessica the other night?"

Jacob blinks at me, his expression unreadable. "What?"

I'm already regretting bringing this up but there's no turning back now. "At the mall? Kaylee Zimmer and Jessica Dolecki?" I clarify, just in case he's confused over which Kaylee and Jessica I'm referring to.

"Yeah, I know who you mean." Now he sounds a little annoyed. "Were you spying on me or something?"

"What? No!" I rush out, shaking my head. "I was at the mall with my mom and I saw you." I fold my arms across my chest, my nails digging into my coat. "It just surprised me, is all. I didn't realize you, uh, were still, um, friends with Jessica."

Jacob's body language has totally changed now. He looks stiff and uncomfortable, and all the laughs we'd shared tonight at the carnival seem to have evaporated.

The silence is so awkward. *Don't say it, don't say it, don't say it. . . .* "So did you guys go there together?" I ask in a small voice, biting my bottom lip. It still tastes like maple. Like Jacob.

"Honestly, Bailey, why does that even matter?" He frowns. "The only way I could see it remotely being something you'd even want to know would be if we were dating each other exclusively. Is that what we're doing?"

"I . . . I haven't really thought about it," I mumble-lie, wishing that the ice rink could suddenly morph into a giant hole that I could throw myself into.

"Well, I guess if we're being open with each other, I'd like to know where things stand," he says, sounding all businesslike about it.

"Are you . . . are you trying to DTR our relationship?" I ask him, incredulous. Here I've been afraid to push the idea of us dating on him—is he actually asking me where things stand? Unreal. And after the past few days, I'm not honestly sure.

He sighs. "I have no idea what that means."

"I guess it means that I'm confused," I say. "You might like me, but maybe . . . maybe you like someone else too."

189

The thing that I couldn't stop thinking about is this: if Jacob could be attracted to an awful person like Jessica, it's hard to reconcile how he'd be attracted to someone like me. We are completely different people (one nice, one not so nice).

Jacob frowns hard. "Are you talking about me or you? I just told you that I like you. Now I'm thinking maybe you're the one who likes someone else."

"That's not it," I protest, though his words hit a nerve. Jacob doesn't know about Charlie—and I want to keep it that way.

"Maybe I should have been following *you* around," he says coldly. "Maybe I'd have learned a few things about you."

Okay, so he definitely doesn't know about Charlie. His words sting a bit, though. I know I don't really have a right to give him a hard time about being at the mall with a couple of girls when I've actually been on bona fide dates with another guy.

A sharp wind whips across the ice rink and straight into my bones. Above us, the strands of twinkling lights tremble.

I shiver, pulling my scarf tighter around my neck. "Look, I don't know why I said anything. I shouldn't have. You can be at the mall with whoever you want. I'm sorry," I say quietly. "I mean it. Can we forget this conversation ever happened?"

Jacob doesn't say anything for a minute. But then his frown turns more into a smirk. He shrugs, rocking back on his heels. "Yeah, sure. We can forget it."

"Okay. Thanks."

He reaches over and takes hold of either end of my scarf. It's a repeat of what Charlie did the other day at the bookstore, except Jacob is undeniably pulling me close to him. "You gotta admit, it's pretty bizarre when you consider we just had our first kiss and our first fight all in the span of five minutes."

"I liked the kissing part better."

"Me too." And he leans over and kisses me again.

19

Merry Christmas, Everybody

"Oh, you guys. I love them!" Mellie trills, holding up two pairs of underpants: one in a camo print, one with unicorns and rainbows. "Seriously, so cute." She studies each of our faces, trying to guess who gifted them. "Hmmmm. I think it was . . . you!" she says, shaking the panties in my direction.

"Stop," I say, laughing. I take a bite of my toasted sesame bagel. We met at the Sunshine Diner for our friend group's traditional preholiday brunch and exchange of gifts. We all dropped them in a tote bag Phoebe brought when we were outside the diner. That way no one knows who brought which gift. "The point of Secret Santa is that it's a secret, Mel," I remind her after I swallow.

Caitlin is cutting her buttermilk pancakes into tiny bite-sized pieces. "Yeah, but you know we always end up telling each other."

"Speak for yourself," Mellie tells her. It's common knowledge that Caitlin is the worst at keeping a secret. The first year we exchanged gifts, we had to do it two weeks before Christmas because Caitlin couldn't stand the wait any longer. She opened her Secret Santa first today. It was a bright green day planner for the new year that came with sticker sheets—a perfect gift for her.

"Shhhh, not yet," Phoebe admonished. She's already unwrapped her fairy lights, and she squealed with joy. If we had an outlet at our table, I wouldn't be surprised if she unboxed them, plugged them in, and put them around her neck like a lei. "Bailey still needs to open hers."

I pull a few crumpled sheets of tissue paper from the gift bag. Inside is a bottle of Essie nail polish in a pretty blue color called Bikini So Teeny . . . and a self-help dating advice book that I've seen at the bookstore: *So, What Are We?: A Girl's Guide to Getting the Love You Deserve.*

"Wow. Thanks, Santa," I say, rolling my eyes at Mellie. She gives me an innocent *What, me?* look and suddenly is fascinated with her omelet.

Caitlin's eyes bop from me to Mellie. "Wait, how do you know Mellie's your Santa?"

I shake my head. "Trust me, I know."

Phoebe picks up the book and examines it. "Is this . . . a relationship book? Who's Bailey in a relationship with?" she asks Mellie and Caitlin, as if I'm not sitting right beside her.

"See, that's the question we need answered," Mellie says thoughtfully, putting her elbows on the table and resting her chin on her closed fists. She bats her eyelashes at me.

I shoot her a warning look. She is the only one I've told about kissing Jacob last night, but I swore her to secrecy. I don't want to talk about it at our brunch. Today is supposed to be about us four—I don't want me and Jacob to be the topic of conversation. My friends always come first. Fries before guys.

"Okay, so you are Bailey's Santa," Caitlin says, oblivious to the daggers coming out of my eyes. "So that means . . . Phoebe? Are you mine?"

Phoebe hesitates, then nods, doing a little dance in her seat. "I know you're always so organized. It just looked like you when I saw it at the store."

"I'm your Santa," Caitlin tells Mellie.

"At this point I kind of assumed that," Mellie says, giving her a hug.

Now that we've all come clean, everyone is relaxed, talking and eating. Caitlin is going to her relatives in Georgia until New Year's, so we won't be seeing much of her over the break. Phoebe is going away, too, but just to Long Island for a few days. Mellie and I are staying local.

I pick up the last crispy strip of bacon on my plate and take a tiny bite. My friends are all laughing and talking, but I feel on the outside of their conversation. I don't want to talk about Jacob. But that doesn't mean I don't want to think about him. It's hard not to. I can't stop reliving our kiss last night . . . or imagining the prospect of kissing him again in the future.

"Are you okay, Bailey?" Phoebe asks, sipping her water. "You seem kind of, I don't know, out of it today."

"I think I know what it is," Mellie says knowingly.

Everyone's eyes zero in on her, including mine. "I think Bailey is struggling to decide what she wants when it comes to a guy," Mellie says slowly. "It's like, she met someone she really likes, but now she's wondering if maybe she could find someone else she likes."

I think about this for a minute. There is a teeny kernel of truth to it. But mostly it's that I've found two people to like. "Okay, Mel. Yep, you got it," I say, trying to end this conversation.

But she isn't about to be shushed that easily. "It's the paradox of choice," she jabbers on. "People always think that the perfect person is waiting for them out there." She throws out her hands expansively. "It's like when you find a perfect match on a dating site. It messes with your head and makes you think that if you found one person, a lot more people are out there who might be right for you."

"Love's just a swipe away," Phoebe agrees.

"I think you're making this harder than it needs to be," Caitlin says. "This guy Charlie seems cool and all, but it sounded pretty friend-zoney. And he doesn't seem that available." Mellie and Phoebe are nodding as she continues. "You told us how much fun you had with Jacob at the Christmas tree farm—the farm his family owns." She laughs as if it's so obvious what I should do, and Mellie and

Phoebe join in. "It doesn't get any more perfect for a Christmas maniac like you, Bailey. Can you say 'destiny'?"

"And he's seriously hot," Mellie adds. "He is!" she says at Phoebe's and Caitlin's looks. "Have you seen his butt?"

"I haven't looked," I tell her, folding my arms, but the blush in my cheeks says otherwise. Pretty soon we're all laughing, and Mellie has started a poll of who has the best butt in the junior class.

I look around the table at their smiling faces. My friends just want what's best for me. But for whatever reason, I just can't make myself open up and tell them how conflicted I am because of Charlie. They'd dissect everything I'd tell them, and I guess maybe I'm afraid there'll be nothing left when they're through.

In my heart, I know what the right choice is. The right choice is the boy who was out there, trying to get to know me—the boy I'd known from afar for years. The boy I wanted to kiss more than anything again.

But saying yes to Jacob means that I'll have to say goodbye to Charlie for good.

And I'm just not ready to do that.

• • •

One year at my sleepaway summer camp, my entire cabin sat in a circle after breakfast and went around identifying our best and worst traits. My counselor, Bri, urged us to be as self-aware as possible. It was a pretty easy activity for me—I've always considered myself to be very self-aware. This means that I also easily knew what my worst trait was—or, at least, a trait I was willing to bring up in front of a group of eleven-year-old girls.

My worst trait is that I often have big ideas but underestimate how long it will take to pull them off. That leads to me putting things off. And that leads to disaster.

The Christmas tree tags is a classic example. My heart was in the right place that day at the senior center . . . but I've procrastinated on doing the shopping, in large part because I'm not sure how I'm going to pay for everything.

The list of things I have to do—have *to buy*—is weighing on me now as I cross the street, my head down. My friends are all going to hang out together at Phoebe's house after brunch, but I told them I have a headache and want to go home and take a nap.

I wasn't lying about the nap part. But I can't just go home and sleep. I have to shop.

"What am I going to do?" I mutter to myself as I head to my car. All the street meters are covered with red holiday shopping bags that say ENJOY THE GIFT OF FREE HOLIDAY SHOPPING. At least I don't have to worry about getting a parking ticket I won't be able to pay for. I shake my head, annoyed with myself. Holiday shopping is supposed to be fun. Enjoyable. Instead, I feel a little sick to my stomach. Everyone whose name is on one of those tags is counting on a gift for Christmas. If they don't receive one, it will be only one person's fault.

Mine.

I start making a mental list of everything I have to buy.

Reya: fabric softener and laundry detergent pods

Jade: blue sweatshirt and sneakers (girls size 4)

Richard: Green queen-sized comforter

Chiara: Yoga mat and leggings size M

Javante: Anything Nike

Sydney: Clothes, size 14

Lost in my thoughts, I'm not paying attention to the sidewalk and I trip over a folded newspaper that was tossed on the pavement. We're always getting circulars in our driveway, stuffed into flimsy plastic bags. This newspaper isn't in a bag, and when my foot kicks it, papers start fluttering out, blowing every which way.

"Shoot," I mumble, chasing after a flyer for a pharmacy and an insert for a window replacement company. Grabbing the papers, I jog back to the newspaper. "You're such a Girl Scout," I mutter, bending down to stick the papers back in the folds of the paper.

And that's when I see it. A plain white envelope—the kind a birthday card comes in—is tucked inside the newspaper. The envelope contents are thick. On the front it says *For You.*

I open the envelope. Inside is a thick wad of twenty- and fifty-dollar bills. "Wait, what?" I gasp, thumbing through the money. There has to be over five hundred dollars here, maybe more. I glance around, wondering if this is some kind of holiday prank. But I'm all alone. "'For you'?" I say, reading aloud the words on the envelope. Does that mean . . . for me?

I know the right thing to do is turn the money in to the police department. If someone had lost this much, they'd definitely report it.

Wouldn't they?

I look at the envelope again. This doesn't seem like someone lost it. It feels almost like someone has left it here, tucked inside a newspaper, hoping someone will find it. My heart starts to race.

Maybe this is my destiny.

Maybe fate or elves or . . . or, okay, I'm not ashamed to consider it, *Santa,* is behind this. It's as if someone knew that I'd be walking by at this very moment, that a gust of wind would send the newspaper pages flying, that I'd stop . . . and that I'd find the envelope.

I'm trying to figure out how to pay for gifts for people who really need them. And then the solution drops into my lap . . . or rather, at my feet.

Maybe turning in the money isn't the right thing to do. This money is the answer to my problem.

I grab the envelope and shove it into my purse before I can talk myself out of it.

Maybe *For You* really does mean . . . for me.

And maybe I'll be able to give a group of very deserving people a very special Christmas.

• • •

I know Jacob is working at the tree farm, so when I get home, I decide to text Charlie, telling him about my good luck and asking him if he wants to help me shop—that I'm not sure I can get everything done on my own. And if I'm being honest, I want to hang out with him one more time. But fifteen minutes have passed, and I still haven't heard from him.

^^^^ I text, which is kind of aggressive, but the clock is ticking.

Suddenly three little dots pop up. I wait.

> Hey . . . that is seriously cool that you found that money. 💸

> I know! I couldn't believe it. 🎉

> I wish I could help you with your shopping list but I'm kind of in the middle of something.

"In the middle of something?" I mutter, wondering what the something is. I sigh. Ahhh, okay. I'm disappointed—but I'm also a little worried. It's one o'clock right now. I only have a few hours to get this done.

> What about your friends? Your family?

> They're busy too. 😞

Even that guy from the other day ... Jacob?

I wince, seeing Jacob's name pop up in Charlie's text. It also feels a little weird for Charlie to bring him up. A guy doesn't bring up another guy to a girl he likes ... does he?

Um, maybe. Okay, thanks. Bye 🌲

I chew nervously on my lip. I don't want to come across as clingy. And maybe I can do this on my own. But shopping is always more fun with a friend—especially a friend with a cute butt.

Hey ... are you still at the farm?

My shift's ending soon. What's up?

I smile as I type. Just playing Santa and I could use your help. How soon can you get here?

• • •

It's 4:00 p.m. on Friday and we're racing around Target like we're on a shopping game show.

"Take it easy, Bailey," Jacob says with a smirk. He's jogging beside me as I weave the shopping cart around people. "You're starting to look a little panicked."

"Oh, this is full-on panic mode," I gasp. "A little panicked was forty minutes ago." We stop short in the laundry detergent aisle, where I find the fabric softener and detergent pods Reya wants. I toss them into the cart. We already found a blue sweatshirt and sneakers for Jade, two cute tops for Sydney, and a neon-green Nike hoodie for Javante.

"Bedding," I wheeze, flinging my arm in the direction we need to go in.

I'm trying not to show it, but I'm still a little salty over how late Jacob was getting to my house. I explained my situation, making it clear time was of the essence. He acted like he'd be right over, but when he finally showed up, it was almost three o'clock. By the time we find all the gifts and get them wrapped, we'll barely make it to the Stewart Center on time. I don't want Louise to worry or think I've forgotten. But it isn't like I can text her. I'll just have to do my best.

"How about this?" Jacob says, holding up what is clearly a twin-sized gray comforter in a clear plastic case. Even worse, it has dinosaurs on it.

"Are you serious? That's a kid's comforter," I say, exasperated. "And it's not even green."

"Does it matter?" Jacob asks, raising his dark eyebrows. "It's a comforter."

"Yes, it matters. First, it's the wrong size." I tap the word *twin*. "And second, it's the wrong color," I say, annoyed. I don't even mention the dinosaurs. Instead, I'm back to scanning the shelves. "We need a green queen-sized comforter," I tell him firmly.

Jacob helps me look. "I don't think you're going to find one," he says, shrugging.

"I have to!" I blurt out, and I feel actual tears spring to my eyes. "You don't understand."

"I understand, but isn't it kinda late?" Jacob asks, looking genuinely perplexed. He picks up a package of pillowcases and tosses it into the air. "Too bad you can't order it online."

"This is Richard's only Christmas gift!" I practically shriek as he catches the package. "He deserves to get what he asked for. Not a stupid gray comforter—or a pair of pillowcases."

I'm losing my cool, but Jacob is staying extra calm. Basically the more frustrated I get, the more chill he appears. Which only increases my frustration. "You probably should have thought about that before you waited until the last minute to go shopping." He holds up his hands. "Just saying."

"Gee, thanks," I say, remembering that day in the café when I told Jacob holiday shopping is stressful only if you wait until the last minute. What a jerk Past Me was!

"I honestly don't need you to tell me that," I continue. "And it would have been nice if you had gotten to my house when you said you'd be there." It's not really fair to blame Jacob for any of this, and he's totally right, but I'm upset. I'm glad he's with me, but I miss the fun, romantic vibe from the other night.

Jacob is silent for a moment. "Yeah, okay." He walks up and down the aisle, scanning the shelves. "Do you want to go somewhere else and see if we can find one?" he asks finally.

I shake my head. He's being so nice to me, and I don't deserve it. "Where? No. It's too late." Now I am starting to cry a little bit. "I have to find something here."

Jacob searches some more, then reaches onto a shelf and pulls out a navy and green rugby-striped comforter. "How about this? It's the right size."

I pause for a moment, and then nod. It isn't quite what I had in mind, but it looks nice. "Great. Yes."

Jacob tosses it into the cart. "Now all you need is the yoga mat and leggings."

To my immense relief, we manage to find them right away, and the line to pay moves really quickly. I pay with the *For You* money and use what's left to buy Louise a gift card.

"Do you need wrapping paper or anything?" Jacob asks as we leave the store and hurry through the parking lot. It's dark out now, and I don't even dare look at my phone to see what time it is.

"No, I'm good," I say, speed-walking to his truck. "All I need is for you to drive fast."

"Relax, Bailey. We're going to make it." For a moment I think he's going to lean over to kiss me, but all he does is reach past me to unlock the truck door.

"Easy for you to say," I tell him as I climb in, my shopping bags banging against my legs. "It's a good thing I know how to wrap fast."

We use my dining room table as a wrapping station and make it to the Stewart Center by 6:46. I don't see Louise—the residents are at a holiday party—but the woman at the front desk promises me she'll give Louise the Christmas card I hand her. The gift card is inside. We leave the gifts on the table, and when we walk out, I heave a gigantic sigh of relief. I didn't realize how tired I am—it's like the stress of the day hits me all at once.

My brother is out with Dickens when we pull up to the curb. "See ya, Bailey," Jacob says, nodding through the window to Liam. Liam nods back.

"Okay. G'night," I say through a yawn.

And before my brother can ask me any questions, I'm in the house.

• • •

I'm curled up now on the couch half watching *Christmas Vacation* with my dad and texting with my friends when I decide to text Jacob. I feel a little bad about how I'd acted. After all, out of all my friends, he is the only one who had made the time to help me.

Hi

Hi

So I just wanted to say thanks for helping me today

But I was late

I wince. I'm sorry I was such a jerk about that. I was just stressed. I really appreciate your time

You're welcome.

Uh-oh. Is he mad? He put a period at the end of the text. Well, thanks. I hope you have a good night ☺

A few minutes go by and he doesn't answer. I feel bad, but I don't know what else I can do. I try to concentrate on the movie, but I have no idea what's happening. I give up and decide to go to bed.

I'm in my pajamas and brushing my teeth in the bathroom I share with Liam and Kar when my phone buzzes, startling me.

Do you want to know why I was late

By the way he's asking me this, I don't think I do. I hesitate, and then type back It doesn't matter

It does

Okay. Tell me

I was at the post office with my mom. She wanted to
pick out a letter from Santa for us to answer on our
way home from the tree farm

My face drops. I spit out a mouthful of toothpaste into
the sink and take a drink of water. OMG. That's so sweet

We were both doing good deeds today

I relax a little. I'm obviously an idiot

You're not an idiot. But maybe next time be a little more chill

No period at the end of his last two texts. I let out a sigh
of relief. I'll try that

And just so you know ... the other night when you saw me at
the mall with Kaylee and Jessica?

I swallow. Yeah?

Jessica doesn't have her driver's license and she heard me
saying that I had to go to the Apple store. She asked me if I could
drive her and Kaylee to the mall. Her mom drove them home

Oh. I frown.

Nothing happened. You must have seen us in the 5 minutes I
stayed with them

I'm sure she was hoping something would happen I type,
then erase it. Thanks for telling me, I write instead. That was
nice of you

I just didn't want you to think something was going on with
Jess. That's a closed door that's never opening again

I so badly want to screenshot this—but I don't. Why
gloat? That's bad karma. Instead, I do a little shimmy on

207

the bathroom rug. I resist the urge to send him the closed door emoji and instead settle for replying with a smiley face.

"Yo, what are you doing in there?" Liam says loudly, thumping insistently on the bathroom door. "Other people would like to shower before midnight, you know."

"Just a sec!" I hastily wipe off the sink with a hand towel and whip the door open so fast my brother blinks in surprise, his arm still raised midknock.

"So sorry," I say briskly, pushing past him as my phone vibrates in my pj pants pocket. "Couldn't find the dental floss."

And when I'm back in the privacy of my room, I read Jacob's last text.

Sweet dreams, Bailey 🖤 🖤 🐧

And I screenshot it.

20

Christmas Is the Time to Say I Love You

Today is Saturday, December 23—the last Saturday before Christmas. Winslow's has had a steady stream of customers—those who special-ordered books, those who are browsing, and those who just came in for some comfort from the cold and for the free hot chocolate Victoria is handing out.

It's always cozy inside here, but today the bookshop feels like a warm hug. Everyone is in a good mood. Even the light snow falling outside makes people happy. "It doesn't feel like Christmas without fresh snow," one of the customers tells me, and I nod happily.

Christmas is finally almost here. And I'm thinking—okay, hoping—that I just might get my underneath-the-mistletoe wish. And I've also come to a decision. As much as it pains me to do it, I've made up my mind to end whatever it is I have with Charlie. No more texting, no more sledding, no more hanging out. It's not that I don't think we could be friends—I know we could. But right now I'm having too much fun with Jacob. I want to see where things might go with him. And it doesn't feel right for me to keep whatever it is I have with Charlie alive.

But still, I'm not prepared when Charlie shows up at the bookstore just when my shift is over and asks if we can talk.

"Um, of course. Sure," I tell him, completely caught off guard. After I exchange goodbye hugs and happy holiday wishes with everyone, I collect my stuff from the back room, including the new Lee Matthews novel I'm borrowing, and put on my coat and hat. Together, we walk outside. There's a small park not far from the bookstore, and that's where we go.

"So listen. I've been a bit dodgy with you. There's something I want to talk to you about," Charlie says when we get there and find a bench. He sits down and pats the space next to him on the bench, brushing off the dusting of snow. "Please, join me."

I sit. "It's kind of weird, because there's something I want to talk to you about too," I tell him, hoping this goes well.

He smiles at me. "Do you want to go first?"

"Not really. But, um, I will." I swallow, trying to gather my thoughts. It's important that I say the right things. "So, I am really glad I got to know you," I begin carefully. "You're a really nice guy, and I've had a lot of fun with you."

"I feel the same," he says, nodding.

I take a deep breath. "Yeah. But the thing is, even though

we've hung out a lot, I don't really feel like I've gotten to know you all that well. It's like everything between us is surface level. We hang out, we have fun, but then we go our separate ways. I'm never sure where things stand."

"That's fair," Charlie says. A lock of hair falls in front of his eye and he blows it off.

I can't get distracted. "It's hard for me to even believe I'm saying this, since you're basically the British boyfriend I've dreamed about for years, but . . . I don't think we should, uh, date each other. Or, um, keep hanging out." There. I said it.

To my surprise, Charlie doesn't look at all surprised. He doesn't look upset or angry or confused. Instead, he looks almost . . . wistful. "I'm glad to hear you say that. Because I feel the same way, Bailey."

I feel the same. I feel the same. Is that all he can say? "You do?" I blurt out, feeling a little dejected. I know that he isn't the right boy for me, but it's demoralizing to hear that he has already put me in the friend zone. "Is that what you came here to talk to me about?"

Charlie shakes his head, his gaze falling, as if there is something I'm not quite understanding. "Don't get me wrong. You're an amazing girl. Any guy would be lucky to have you as a girlfriend. But . . ."

"What . . . ?" I prompt.

He sighs. "The thing is, I try not to get too close to people." He looks up at me, his eyes staring into mine. "But there's a reason for that, Bailey."

I tilt my head and wait to hear what it is.

He's on the verge of saying something—and then he stops. "You have a great family, right?"

"Um, yeah," I say, not sure where this is going. "What does that have to do with anything?"

He brushes my question off. "And loyal friends who always have your back?"

I nod. "Ride or die."

He points to a man walking a beagle down the path. "And a dog who adores you?"

I make a face. "*Adore* is a strong word. But fine, sure," I say, going along with him. Where is this all leading?

The streetlamps have flicked on, and snow is starting to fall a bit heavier now, the light capturing the snowflakes like winter fireflies. "You've got a family, friends, a home, good health—all the things that people want out of life."

"Does this have something to do with the gifts I dropped off at the Stewart Center?" I ask suddenly. "Did I forget someone?" I smack my head. "I can't believe this. I double-checked that list—"

"It's not about the Stewart Center." Charlie reaches over and takes my hands in his. I feel a warm tingle in my palms, like a faint jolt of electricity. "What's your favorite movie?" he asks me.

"*It's a Wonderful Life*," I answer, and he smiles, like he already knew I was going to say it.

"It's a classic," Charlie says. "It's why you're named Bailey, isn't it?"

"Yeah." I sit back a little. "You're one of the only people who's ever figured that out. My parents love that movie. Liam got a family name, but then it was all up for grabs. If I'd been a boy, my parents wanted to name me Harry after Harry Bailey, George Bailey's younger brother—"

"—the one who falls in the ice and grows up to be a war hero," Charlie finishes.

"Yep. And my younger sister is named after one of the actresses in the movie." I let out a wistful sigh. "If only they'd named her Zuzu . . . that would have been so good."

Now Charlie laughs. "Your sister got lucky." He grows quiet for a moment. Snow has blanketed the ground, and the air feels completely still and silent. We're now completely alone in the park. "The thing is . . . what I was trying to say is . . . I'm glad you don't want to date me."

Oof. "Um, wow. Okay. Thanks for the honesty," I tell him. "But you seriously made a special trip over here just to tell me that?"

He shakes his head again, as if I'm not getting it. "No, it's not like that. I'm going to be going away, sort of, and—" He breaks off. "Just hear me out, Bailey. Remember the day we met? And that night, how it was snowing so hard it was a whiteout?"

I nod. "Yes. Of course I remember."

"At the ice rink, I was just there to observe—but when you almost fell, I got involved. I knew what was supposed to happen later, and I wanted it to play out the way it was supposed to."

I shake my head, confused. He isn't making any sense.

Charlie goes on. "That night, you got stuck in that snowbank," he went on. "If I hadn't come along when I did, a 1972 F100 Ford truck would have."

Huh? That's the truck Jacob drives. I shake my head. "I'm not understanding where you're going with this. If you hadn't stopped to help me, Jacob Marley would have?" And how the heck does Charlie know what kind of truck Jacob has?

"No." Charlie's still holding my hands, and he pulls me closer, an earnest expression on his face. "Bailey, it was your crucial night. If I didn't stop to help you and get you on your way, something bad would have happened—Jacob Marley would have left Joe Shiffley's party. Upset over not talking to you, he would be driving too fast and playing his music too loud. In that whiteout, he wouldn't have seen your car in time to stop. He would have hit you. You both—" Charlie shakes his head. "I couldn't let that happen."

I'm still as a statue. "We both *what?* And what do you mean, *let that happen?*"

Charlie squeezes my hands. "Bailey Briggs, named after George Bailey and believer in Christmas Magic, don't you get it?" he asks quietly.

"Can you spell it out for me?" I whisper, my voice cracking. "Because I think I do get it and I'm slightly freaked out right now."

Charlie lets go of my hands and rests his palms on top of my trembling shoulders. "I've been given a great gift, Bailey.

I get to watch out for you and protect you and help you. I'm—"

"Stop! Don't say it," I cry out, holding my hand across his mouth. If he says what I think he's going to say, that would mean he has serious mental issues . . . or it would mean that he is . . . an angel.

This is not something I'm prepared to deal with after my twelve-to-six shift at Winslow's.

"I thought you wanted me to 'spell it out for you,'" he says, using air quotes.

"Changed my mind," I say firmly. But then a calmness comes over me and I realize . . . as crazy as it is, I believe him.

From the moment I first laid eyes on Charlie that day at the ice rink, there was something about him that felt special and different. And now I know why. Suddenly it all makes sense—the snowbank, the beautiful cookies, the tree tags, the North Pole. . . .

Everything falls into place, like the last piece in the Christmas puzzle my family works on each year. It's like the holiday sign my mom hangs up in our family room. JUST BELIEVE.

And I do.

"There's a reason both you and Jacob were spared that night," he tells me, and I'm hanging on his every word. "You're going to do important things in your lives. You both have to be alive for those things to happen."

"So we end up together?" I let out a little gasp. "We get . . .

married?" I like Jacob—I like him a lot—but I am not ready for this level of commitment. I'm only a high school junior!

Charlie laughs. "Slow your roll there, Bailey. Focus on the here and now. That's what's important. You have a wonderful life ahead of you. And so does Jacob. I just needed to make sure you each had the opportunity to live it."

21

Mistletoe

"You look really pretty," Jacob says, his voice soft. It's finally my favorite night of the year, Christmas Eve, and here is my favorite guy, standing in my living room.

It's like a dream.

"So do you." Then we both laugh. "You know what I mean," I say, blushing. He looks great. He has on dark jeans, and a sweater over a dress shirt. And he got a haircut, but it's just a trim, barely noticeable if you aren't paying attention. I'm wearing a cream sweater and skirt, with little rhinestone barrettes pulling back my hair on either side of my face. Without my boots on, he is a good four or five inches taller than me.

My family is in the middle of getting ready for our traditional Christmas Eve feast with all my aunts and uncles and cousins. My aunt Amy hosts every year, and my family is upstairs getting ready. Jacob has a family dinner to go to as well. But when he called to ask if he could come over for a little while, of course I said yes. I've never gotten ready so fast.

Snow is falling outside our window, and our neighborhood is aglow in holiday lights. It's magical. A fire is crackling in the fireplace, and our Christmas tree looks beautiful, its white lights twinkling. Dickens is underneath it, nestled between presents, chewing on a toy bone Jacob brought him. And Liam's laptop is on the coffee table, open to noradsanta.org so we can track Santa's progress across the globe. He's just been spotted over Azerbaijan.

"Nice tree you have there," Jacob says, grinning. "How's the one from the farm doing?"

"Oh, it's great," I say. "I have it up in my room. I went with a candy theme—the whole tree is decorated with ornaments like cake slices and lollipops."

"That's . . . sweet."

I give him a good-natured sock in the arm. "Ouch, that hurt," he kids, and I reach over and squeeze his biceps. It feels good to joke around with him. I can't stop smiling.

"So I got you something, and I wanted to give it to you before tomorrow," Jacob tells me. He walks over to where he left his coat and comes back with a small gift-wrapped box. He places it in my hands.

"Should I open it now?" I ask, excited. I still can't believe he's at my house, let alone giving me a Christmas present. Luckily I have one for him too—a customized paint-by-numbers painting of Wags I ordered on Etsy. It's wrapped and under the tree in—no surprise—the Dogs in Stockings gift wrap.

He nods. Inside the box is a delicate gold chain with a slim gold bar at the center. On the bar is a series of numbers. I squint to read them in the firelight.

"It's the coordinates of the bookstore," Jacob says, and I can tell how excited he is to give it to me. "I know it's a special place to you. And it's special to me, too, because it's where we met, not counting school."

"I love it," I breathe, holding it up. "Would you put it on me?" It's the most thoughtful gift I've ever received.

Jacob stands behind me and fastens the clasp while I hold up my hair. "Do you like it?"

"It's perfect." I turn to face him. After my conversation with Charlie last night, I'm looking at Jacob with new eyes. Everything about him seems clearer and brighter—and not just because it's Christmas Eve. I wish I could tell him about Charlie, about how he saved both our lives, how he told me we were destined to do great things, but I know I can't.

When we said goodbye last night, I understood that I wasn't going to see Charlie anymore—maybe not ever. But I also instinctively know that he'll always be there, hovering around the edges, ready to swoop in if I need him. I am going to miss him.

Now it's time to appreciate what I have right in front of me. Real-life Christmas Magic.

Jacob reaches into his back pocket and takes out a little

green sprig dotted with white berries. "I brought this from the farm," he says. "I tried not to bend it."

"Is that actual mistletoe?" I ask, my breath catching in my throat. My wish is coming true before my eyes.

"It's the real deal," he says quietly. "You are, too, Bailey. I think you're amazing. Will you . . . will you be my girlfriend?" He holds the mistletoe over our heads, and I lean in to kiss him.

"I would have done that without the mistletoe, you know," I whisper.

"Just wanted to be prepared," he says, wrapping his other arm around me and pulling me close. "Merry Christmas, Bailey."

"Merry Christmas, Jacob."

And maybe it is my imagination, but as our lips touch, I'm pretty sure I hear a sleigh bell ring.

Acknowledgments

The Nice List

Everyone at Underlined: my editor, Kelsey Horton, who made my story merry and bright; art director Alison Impey, who went the extra holiday mile for me; Josie Portillo, for a holly jolly cover; Lili Feinberg, Colleen Fellingham, Marla Garfield, Erica Henegen, Jenn Inzetta, Alison Romig, Tamar Schwartz, and Elizabeth Ward for their goodwill and good cheer; and a cup o' kindness to Beverly Horowitz.

My dear friends who keep the season bright.

My family, for making every single Christmas the best one ever.

And in loving memory of Dickens, the best dog and truest friend.

Get swept away in another
Underlined romance!

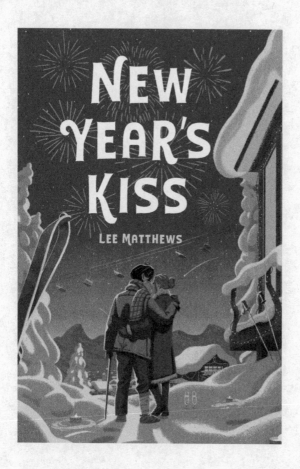

CHAPTER ONE

DECEMBER 26

"It looks like a drunk elf threw up in here."

I snorted a laugh and looked at my sister, Lauren, as we stopped just inside the sliding glass doors to the Evergreen Lodge. Lauren was not wrong. The huge, three-story lobby atrium, with its exposed wood beams and tremendous chandeliers (made of a thousand fake deer antlers), was still decorated for Christmas—and the sensory experience was an onslaught of yuletide cheer. Every one of the beams was swagged with evergreen garland and roped with white twinkle lights. The chandeliers had been draped in red-and-green-plaid ribbon, and large glass balls hung overhead. Christmas-themed pillows overflowed from every couch and chair, and there were Christmas trees of all sizes everywhere. In the corners, on the counters, acting as centerpieces for the low coffee tables. There was even a life-sized animatronic Santa next to the check-in desk, waving with one hand and holding a plate of cookies in the other, while the instrumental soundtrack to *The Nutcracker* played at a respectful volume from hidden surround-sound speakers.

"Why does the elf have to be drunk?" I asked.

Lauren rolled her eyes like I was *so* lame. Which, let's be honest, I should be used to by now. But my cheeks went ahead and started burning anyway. Lauren pretty much always thought I was lame. I wasn't sure why I kept trying. If there was one thing for certain on this earth, it was that my big sister and I did *not* share the same sense of humor. Or style. Or basic outlook on life. And still . . .

"No, seriously," I said. "Couldn't the elf just have the flu? Or E. coli?"

"Ew!" Lauren scrunched her perfect nose. "That's so gross."

"How is throwing up from the flu grosser than throwing up from being drunk? Barf is barf."

"Why do you always do this?" Lauren asked.

I have no idea, I thought.

"Do what?" I said.

"Overanalyze everything. It was just an offhanded joke. God, Tess. Just chill."

Lauren sighed the sigh of the world-weary and looked at her phone, punching in a message with her thumbs before shoving it back into the pocket of her tight jeans. The second she looked up, she shouted "Loretta!" and raised her arm straight up in the air. Her smile even seemed genuine, which was impressive, considering Lauren had spent the entire shuttle ride over from the tiny regional airport bitching about how our grandmother—who had insisted we call her Loretta from the day each of us could talk—hadn't sent a car. Instead, we had been jammed into the back of the twelve-seat Evergreen Lodge minibus with ten other ski-obsessed Vermont vacationers, all of whom had been in far better, louder, and even singier moods than we had. "Twelve Days of Christmas" was going to be playing on repeat in my head until basically the end of time.

"Girls!" Loretta called, walking over to us in her high heels and pencil skirt. Her chic steel-gray bob gleamed under the lights, and her makeup was, as always, perfectly applied—cheekbones defined, lips outlined, eyelashes long and curled. She air-kissed first Lauren, then me—enveloping us in a cloud of her rose-scented perfume—then stepped back to look us over.

Loretta was wearing a white silk shirt, a pearl choker, and tasteful diamond earrings. She looked like a million bucks, as usual. I tugged at the frayed cuffs of my sweatshirt and wondered if any of my friends' grandmothers made them feel frumpy and unstylish like mine did. Wasn't it supposed to be the other way around? My other grandma—Nana, my mom's mom—was twenty pounds heavier than Loretta, wore nothing but colorful cotton sweaters and jeans, and smelled of apple pie and Bengay. *She* made me feel ready for Fashion Week.

Not that I had put in maximum effort this morning. The day after the worst Christmas ever, and I was getting on a plane with my sister to enjoy a week of exile. If any day had ever screamed "comfy sweats," it was this one.

"Oh, it's good to see you both," Loretta said. "How was your trip?"

"It was fine," I told her just as Lauren said, "It was long." This was true. We'd had to fly from Philadelphia to Boston, hang out in the airport there for over an hour, and then board the tiny plane over to the Stowe airport, where we'd gotten on the musical shuttle bus. But I'd never been one to complain.

"Well, you're here now. Just wait until you see all the incredible events the staff has planned for this week. You girls are going to have such a fabulous time."

Lauren looked at me out of the corner of her eye, and I had to look away to keep from laughing again. There was always a litany of "incredible events" planned at Evergreen Lodge. My dad's family had run the place for generations, with Loretta at the helm now. The lodge was more like a compound, consisting of the main building with its huge lobby, event spaces, restaurants and coffee bar, indoor pool, fully equipped gym, and one hundred hotel-style rooms. But it didn't end there. Several outbuildings housed a spa, a greenhouse, a boathouse, a wedding chapel, a dance hall, a couple dozen private cabins, and the Little Green Lodge at the top of the ski lifts where people could rest and get hot chocolate and snacks between runs. Plus there was a staff of hundreds, each with their own specialty, whether it be lifeguarding, line-dancing, or fireside storytelling. Loretta knew every member of the staff by name and treated them all like family. Which was to say, she smiled at them occasionally.

Evergreen Lodge reminded me of this movie called *Dirty Dancing,* which my mom had made both me and Lauren watch the second we turned twelve. It had been Mom's favorite movie as a kid, and sometimes I wondered if that movie was the entire reason my mother had fallen in love with my dad. She must have walked into Evergreen Lodge the first time and envisioned Baby and Johnny doing their iconic lift in the center of the lobby and just said, *That's it! I'm in!* Of course, Mom and Dad's romance hadn't worked out quite as well as the one depicted in the movie. My parents were currently in the midst of finalizing their divorce. Which was the entire reason Lauren and I were here. Usually we came in the summer, because my mom liked hiking better than skiing, but we'd been here a few times in February so that Lauren and I could learn to ski, which was one of my dad's favorite things. This was the first time I had seen the place all done up for the holidays, though. Normally, I loved Christmas and would relish this cozy, merry atmosphere. With the way things were in my life right now, though, I was not in the mood.

Christmas was over, and I sort of wished the staff had already de-merried the place.

A family of four walked through the doors behind us, toting their skis and snowboards, the parents laughing and holding hands with ruddy faces and windswept hair. My heart panged. How could people be walking around all happy and carefree when everything was falling apart?

"Let's get you two settled," Loretta said, clasping her hands. She pivoted on her heel and led us across the lobby. "I've reserved one of the bigger rooms on the third floor for you. It has fantastic views of the mountains and the lake—not that I expect you'll be spending much time in your room, what with everything going on around the resort."

"Wait. *Our* room?" Lauren said. "As in *one* room?"

"Yes, I reserved just the one this time," Loretta said, glancing back over her shoulder at us with an expression that told us there would be no arguments. "Your parents thought it would be good for the two of you to spend some time together. You know, family time."

Heat flared through my entire body. How hypocritical could our parents be? Right now, at this very moment, they were literally splitting up our family. They had shipped us off the day after Christmas for the express purpose of dividing their things, boxing up my dad's stuff, *moving him out.* Because of them, there would never be *family time* again. So why did Lauren and I have to suffer?

"You've got to be kidding me," Lauren scoffed. "Do you have any idea how hypocritical that is?"

"Lauren!" I scolded under my breath, though I was more annoyed that my sister had the guts to say what I didn't.

"What? You know it's true," Lauren said as we stepped into the elevator. There was a giant wreath hung on the back wall, full of glittering berries and fake cardinals. An instrumental version of "It's Beginning to Look a Lot Like Christmas" played through the overhead speakers.

Loretta hit the button for the third floor and sniffed. "Girls, whatever your thoughts on your parents' current situation, you must understand this is difficult for them, too. They're both doing the best they can."

If throwing us out and forcing us to share the same room for a week is the best they can do, then we have serious problems, I thought.

I glanced at Loretta. Maybe I could ask my grandmother if I could come live with her. Maybe if I spent my last year and a half of high school with Loretta, I'd become poised and sophisticated by osmosis. And one day I could take over Evergreen Lodge and run the ice-skating competitions each January and the s'mores-and-scares campfire nights at Halloween, and the movies under the stars on summer weekends.

Loretta looked back at me. "We should get you an appointment at the salon while you're here, Tess. I don't know what's going on with that hair."

Lauren laughed.

Or maybe not.

...

It wasn't as if I didn't want to be more like my sister. In certain ways, anyway. I would have killed to have that seemingly effortless beauty of hers—to look fresh-faced and pretty without a hair out of place at all times—but for me, it was just impossible. Lauren took after our mom, having inherited her gorgeous olive complexion, lustrous dark hair, and natural curves. I, however, looked just like our Irish dad, with skin so white I practically glowed in the dark and very blah dark blond hair. Even on those rare days when I did manage to get my perfectly straight locks to look sleek and healthy before leaving the house, by the time I hit the bathroom after homeroom it was all piece-y and lanky and just hung there. While Lauren walked around looking like she had just stepped off a yacht somewhere in the Greek isles, I looked more like I'd just come from the potato fields and a hard day's work.

Such was the genetic roulette wheel, I guessed. I mean, we'd learned all about it in bio at the beginning of the year. I knew it was no one's fault. But that didn't change the fact that it sucked. And it sucked even harder that my dear old grandmother felt the need to point out my flaws. Especially when those very flaws had come from *her* side of the family, thank you very much.

"You two get settled and I'll see you down in the Antelope Room for dinner in a bit."

"Thanks, Loretta," I said gamely as our grandmother silently closed the door.

Lauren tossed her suitcase onto the double bed nearer the bathroom and groaned. "I can*not* believe we have to share a room for the next week." She pulled out her phone and started texting. "No offense."

I rolled my eyes and wheeled my suitcase over to the dresser to start unpacking my clothes. Even when we were on vacation, I liked to feel settled and organized, while Lauren preferred to live out of her suitcase like she was already on her planned gap year in Europe, where she intended to stay at Airbnbs or with any friends lucky enough to be studying abroad freshman year and "live life like it was intended to be lived," whatever that meant. I couldn't even imagine flying to a foreign country by myself, let alone cobbling together an itinerary *and* finding ways to earn money on the fly. I'd started babysitting the second I was old enough and had been stashing away twenty percent of everything I made ever since, saving up for college textbooks. My parents were always moaning and groaning about how paying for college wasn't about just the tuition but all the living expenses and supplies—especially the books. The way they talked, you'd think textbooks were all made of diamonds and gold.

I had no idea whether my parents' divorce was going to affect the family's money situation, or Lauren's and my college funds, but there was no way I was not going away to school. If there was anything I could do to help make it happen, I would. Traveling the world was all well and good for Lauren, but I was about schedules and goals and ticking off syllabus boxes. I couldn't wait to be in a place where everyone was focused on learning.

Once I'd gotten everything neatly placed inside the dresser, I zipped up my suitcase again, shoved it in a corner, and turned to gaze out the huge picture window overlooking the grounds. The sun was just setting over the mountains, turning the winter sky the most intense shade of pink I'd ever seen. Just below, dozens of people skated around the frozen lake, little kids grabbing onto parents' legs, older kids chasing one another and biffing spectacularly. A couple near the center held hands and twirled in a fast circle, using centrifugal force to keep them going. It was all very pretty, so I took a deep breath and attempted to smile. Unfortunately, I couldn't quite pull it off.

Irritated, I yanked the heavy curtains closed. That was when I spotted a printed schedule on the polished oak desk, a piece of furniture they'd stuck in every room, I supposed because of all the business retreats the lodge hosted. With a glance, I saw that it was a calendar of all the events Loretta had alluded to in the lobby. Everything from a timed snowman-building competition to a snowshoe race. Certain items had been highlighted in green, with a little *M* written next to them in Loretta's stiff handwriting. It was a lovely schedule, really—color-coded by age range for each event with the start and end times indicated. Just my kind of document.

"What do you think this means?" I asked, walking over to Lauren's bed. My sister was now kicked back against the pillows, watching music videos on YouTube.

"What?" Lauren asked without moving her eyes off the screen.

I grabbed her phone—"Hey!" she yelled—and shoved the paper in front of her face.

"This. What do you think the *M*s mean?"

Lauren snatched the page from my hand and scanned it, squinting. "International Buffet, New Year's Eve Teen Dance, Campfire Bingo . . . all marked with an *M*." She slapped the paper down dramatically and looked up at me. "You don't think she means *mandatory*, do you?"

"Oh, no. No way," I said. "I plan to spend the next six days in this room, reading and watching TV."

"There's a shock," Lauren said sarcastically.

"You're the one who was just watching YouTube!" I shot back.

"I was relaxing for five minutes, not hermit-ing myself away for *days*." Lauren got up and pulled off her sweater, which she tossed onto the floor in a heap. "I'm going to get out of here as soon as possible. But if Loretta thinks it's going to be so I can . . . 'build gingerbread houses,'" she read off the list, making a disgusted face, "she's out of her mind."

Actually, building gingerbread houses sounded kind of fun. My dad and I used to make them every Christmas when I was little—from a kit, but still. I loved planning out the decorations for our house and using the squeeze bag of icing to attach the candies (the ones I didn't eat). Suddenly I missed my dad so much my chest hurt.

Why was Mom making him leave? Why couldn't she just try harder?

"I don't know what your problem is," Lauren said, looking over the calendar again. "Don't you just *love* to have every moment of your life scheduled?"

Okay. She had a point. If I were in any mood for festive holiday fun, I would be all about this calendar of events, especially the mandatory parts. Honestly, even as I stood there, the idea was beginning to grow on me.